Devastated Lands
A Post-Apocalyptic Adventure
Bruce W. Perry

D1711348

Acknowledgement

I am indebted to the following U.S.G.S. web site for research on this novel's plot and adventure narrative: U.S.G.S. Volcano Hazards Program (https://volcanoes.usgs.gov/volcanoes/mount_rainier/geo_hist_summary.html)–and related pages, including the Cascades Volcano Observatory (https://volcanoes.usgs.gov/observatories/cvo/)

Lahar: "Lahar is an Indonesian term that describes a hot or cold mixture of water and rock fragments that flows down the slopes of a volcano and typically enters a river valley." –https://volcanoes.usgs.gov/vhp/lahars.html

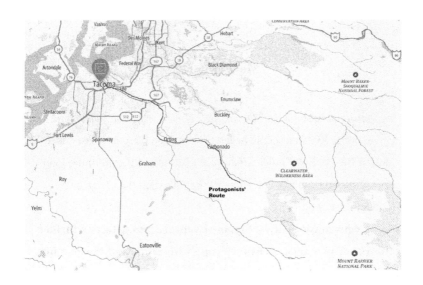

More Fiction

Tsunami Beach, Book 2 of *Devastated Lands*. Mikaela, Shane, and Amy Cooper live in a scenic beach town on the Oregon Coast called Cannon Beach. Sixty miles offshore is a stretch of the 600-mile long mega-thrust earthquake and tsunami region called the Cascadia Subduction Zone
(CSZ). **This mashup of dystopian adventure and detective thriller follows our protagonists as they cope with crime and the looming threat of natural disaster!**

The Last **Emma Blair, a Scottish national, is a pandemic research scientist for the World Health Organization in New York City, where a highly transmissible and virulent form of influenza A decimates the city and spreads throughout world capitals. "The Last" is part dystopian survival adventure and part medical mystery**!

Atomic Night A "desert noir" that takes place mostly in Palm Springs and the desert. The first book in the Chad Kidd crime thriller series. ...**Terrific thriller...Atmospheric...Compelling and Memorable Characters**...*IndieReader on first edition Atomic Night*, March, 2019.

To The North The explosion of the Yellowstone calderas inspires a man to launch a quixotic journey, in response to a faint cry for help over a functioning network. **"Reminiscent of Cormac McCarthy... heart-wrenching...masterful...evocative...",** *Self Publishing Review, 2018*

Accidental Exiles **A young Iraq veteran flees the Middle Eastern wars to Europe**–available in paperback and ebook. "A genuine pleasure to read. It is hard not to respect any author who is able to capture the terror and heartbreaking nature of war, while also detailing the delicate heartbreak of missed chances and lost love, and Perry achieves both with a deftly-subtle hand. The tone is consistent, the pacing is perfect, and the plot is striking in a way that fiction often lacks." *Self Publishing Review,* 2017

CHAPTER 1

Shane lay on a hillside and scanned the gray, denuded scene through the crossbow's scope. Crickets chirped, wind soughed through grass, but nothing moved. The empty meadow was bordered by withered, toppled-over trees.

A debris field and cooled lahar stretched to the horizon, like a giant soiled glacier that wasn't there two weeks ago. The air carried a charred, sulfurous odor.

He unscrewed the scope from the bow, which had a handgrip like a rifle's. Then he carefully slipped the scope back into the rucksack. He lay back against the pack to rest. He was starved and feeling lean, but he figured the vast majority of wildlife had either been wiped out or driven by fear to miles distant.

Although well hidden in the remaining tall grasses, Shane Cooper didn't let himself fall completely asleep. Not in the daylight. Not after what he'd seen in the shattered neighborhood just after dropping into the Puyallup Valley.

The silence was broken by the sound of squeaking

1

wheels in need of lubricating oil. It came from farther up the road, around a bend.

In all the time he had spent in the mountains, Shane had developed a habit of preparation; a healthy paranoia that was now, in retrospect, justified. He'd taken his crossbow and Swiss Army knife with him, even on errands to fetch milk and butter.

Back home, he kept the rucksack packed with essentials in his truck; food, water, powerful flashlight, a first-aid kit. Now he carried those with him.

He'd known he wouldn't be able to predict when he would need them—society seemed frail, shaky, poised to teeter and collapse. He wanted to be able to move and protect himself when the time did come. He used to think about how mad at himself he'd be if the time arrived and caught him unprepared.

Shane lived in a one-story cabin outside of Telluride, Colorado, high in the Rockies. He did mountain guiding for climbers, skiers, photographers, and tourists (he wasn't a hunting kind of guy). Once in a while, he'd be asked to join bigger guiding outfits, and that's what had brought him this time to the Pacific Northwest.

He owned a gun, a repeating Winchester. It hung on a wall in his cabin. He did not have that for hunting, because he didn't shoot wildlife for sport. He figured he shared the Rocky Mountains around Telluride with them, and only the necessity to hunt for sustenance would ever change his mind. Like now.

At any rate, he liked the bow better than a rifle. It was quieter; it didn't give his position away. His stomach growled as he stood up and hoisted the pack onto his shoulders. Odorous vapors from fires and eruptions drifted over the hillsides.

He wanted to head east, away from the devastation at Rainier. He knew it could erupt again at any moment, toasting him in a way he was only lucky it didn't the first time around.

He removed the scope again and put it to his eye, sweeping the countryside and road. He spotted a slumped-over

2

man pushing a shopping cart. A small girl strolled next to him. The clattering, squeaky wheels made them louder than they were visible, a dangerous proposition, Cooper thought. It gave away their position and made them easy prey.

The man and his motley possessions came into focus through the scope. A leash strung from the front of the cart, and at the end of it strained a big dog, partly a black lab, he thought. The little girl had long dirty blond hair and a plain dress. She fairly skipped along.

Cooper watched them continue, then around the corner and out of sight. The guy, with scraggly hair, a long beard, and muddy clothes hanging off his body, seemed more desperate than Cooper was. He figured he'd let him wander out of sight, with who was probably his daughter, before Cooper headed east through the battered forests.

He walked down the hill toward the road, figuring he'd take that route as the sun went down, when he heard men yelling. The dog barking; a little girl's scream. Cooper turned back west and ran up the opposite hillside.

CHAPTER 2

He reached the top of the hill, which was bare and covered in black tree stumps. He knelt down and surveyed the scene below. There were two men in dirty, dark-green fatigues, and black head gear. They held the skinny man roughly by a loose sleeve. A Jeep was parked nearby. They seemed to interrogate the man, pointing to his cart and its contents.

The little girl squatted off to the side, her hands over her ears, as if to block out the conversation. The dog, tensed, its ears perked up, stood at the end of his leash.

They definitely were not National Guard, Cooper figured, with their soiled and rotten aspects. They'd chalked up their faces with a white, floury get-up, like college students at a basketball game.

The Guard was supposed to be patrolling the countryside, but he hadn't seen any since the eruption. Nothing official, that is.

The man who owned the cart then pulled his arm away from the interrogator, as though he'd had enough. He

4

attempted to back away. He seemed to be pleading, both palms upturned. The second thug lurched forward and wrestled the skinny man to the ground. Then he stood up and put a heavy foot on him so he couldn't move. The other man removed a machete from a sheaf he had strapped around his shoulder.

The girl stood up, crept to the cart, and silently loosened the leash on it. *Clever*, Cooper whispered. When the dog sensed his freedom, he bolted, heading west on the crumbled road. Cooper watched but stayed out of sight.

"Kill the dog!" the bandanna-ed man yelled gruffly to his stout accomplice. That man lit off in pursuit of both the dog and the girl, who ran down the road calling out the name, which sounded to Cooper, still at least 50 meters away, like "Burt!"

The man with the machete had it pointed at the throat of the skinny fellow, who seemed to be trying to reason with him. Cooper saw him put his hand between his throat and the sharp end of the machete. Then the scope's lens rose and magnified the big man in dirty fatigues who loped heavily down the road, almost reaching the girl. Her hair flowed behind her. He grabbed her by the locks. She looked back at him with wide-eyed fright; she screamed. Cooper moved about 10 meters closer to get in better position. She desperately reached back toward the lout's big greasy hand to pull it away.

Cooper watched the arrow leave his bow, the wire grow taut again. He could see the silver projectile against the sky, before seconds later it struck the lout solidly, a center shot, knocking him right off his feet, just as if Cooper had shoved him hard from behind. The man collapsed on the side of the road. Cooper didn't take his eye off the lens. The little girl paused, looked down at the pinioned man with a wonder, at the protection that came from the sky. Then she turned and ran in pursuit of the dog.

Cooper stood up and aimed the scope farther up the road. The skinny man lay on the ground, while the other thug scanned the hillside just to Cooper's north, trying to determine the origin of the arrow. He'd seen the arrow pierce his companion. Cooper didn't give him a second more of time. He rearmed, placed the crosshairs on the man's chest, took a deep breath, released. The "pffft!" was the only sound on the remnants of the burned hill, when as if by magic, an arrow stuck out from the man's left breast plate, piercing the fatigue cloth as if it was aimed by a laser. He pitched backward, then lay and writhed next to the cart pusher. There, on the empty road, he died.

Cooper could see the little girl running in the distance. He gathered his gear, stored it in the rucksack, then trotted down the hill to the road.

The scruffy man who'd been pushing his cart had been killed by a bloody blow to the head. Cooper bent over and roughy reclaimed his arrow from the body of the machete killer, then made his way quickly down the road. The big man with the black kerchief tied around his head lay slumped on the side of the road, with a white-powdered scowl. The white tribal get-up made both of the men seem atavistic–a tribe that'd escaped from a crack in the earth, just like the lahar had.

When Cooper reached the top of the hill, he saw her in a field, calling for the dog.

The defensive killing made him feel reckless, jittery, and wild; a fatigue of aftermath settled over him. It wasn't something that exactly came natural, although he accepted his accuracy with the crossbow as a necessary survival skill.

He needed water; his lips were dried and cracked. Likely, they all needed water and food. He walked fifty yards into a meadow with tall grass, straw-colored weeds and shriveled purple and yellow flowers. They made him think of the Rockies, in Fall.

The girl turned and looked at him warily. As far as she knows, he thought, I'm just another threat, who's only standing on top of the heap of threats, for the moment.

"Do you see him?" Cooper called out.

"Who?"

"Your doggie."

"No," she said, wiping away a tear. The breeze blew

6

through the flowers, which came up past her calico dress.

"I can find him," he said, scanning the dark woods that bordered the hills and the road. "What's his name?"

"Turk," she said, and looked away.

"Turk! Turk!" Cooper called out, but he couldn't see anything yet.

"Darn," he muttered. "Which way did he go? Where did you last see him?"

She pointed in the direction of the forest.

"Turk!" he called again, cupping his hands around his mouth, walking towards the woods. "Here boy!" After hesitating, the girl followed him. She stayed a safe distance.

"That fella, with the shopping cart, was that your daddy?" She had a distant look, escaping somewhere into a nicer zone. He couldn't blame her, a kid outside in this lawless, loveless maelstrom.

"That's Eddy," she said after a minute, then she looked behind her. "Where's Eddy?" She said it almost as an afterthought.

"So, he isn't your daddy?"

"Nah," she said. "He was just looking after me." *Good*, Cooper thought. He wasn't very good at the comforting skills; he had no children of his own. He'd never had to do comforting before.

"Where *is* he?" she said, scrunching up her face. When he didn't reply, she said, "Is Eddy dead?"

"Yeah, he is."

"Oh."

"Did you give the doggie his name? Turk?" he said, to change the subject. "It's an interesting name."

"No, he likes turkey. For his lunch. Get it? Turk...turkey...you silly!" Cooper laughed, and *that* felt nice, releasing a warm surge inside. It had been a while. He wanted to completely lose it, with laughter. Then he saw the dog, wandering out from the edge of the woods.

"Hey, there he is! Turk! Turk!"

"C'mere Turk!" she yelled. The dog loped across the

meadow toward them, disappearing and reappearing above the plants, dangling his leash. Cooper gazed over the emptied, flattened houses, the fields, and the gray, dirty lahar, which curled away like a rubberized blot on the landscape. He, the dog, and the girl seemed alone, for now.

CHAPTER 3

They bounced along the dusty road in the Jeep. It had
no top; the girl sat in the front seat beside him. Turk, nose to
the wind, ears flapping, sat behind them, along with their few
belongings. Cooper had found the Jeep's keys on one of the
pinioned bodies. When the girl wasn't looking, he'd dragged
Eddy's body into the bushes. The effort seemed crude and
bleak. Under different circumstances, he would want to
properly bury him. Now he was looking after this little girl;
he'd felt he didn't have the wherewithal to bury the man's
body.

They headed west, toward the coast and Puget Sound,
against his best judgement. East, away from the Cascade
mountains, and the chaos, was where he wanted to go. She
claimed her parents lived a couple of towns over, toward
Tacoma and Seattle, so he gave in.

We have to find Millie, she'd said.
Who's Millie? Your Mom?
Yeah.

She's with your dad? What's his name?
Tom. We have to find Millie and Tom.

They bumped along the road. "What's that?" she said, pointing to the steaming path of destruction, as if she'd just noticed it. The remnants of the lahar was barely a half mile away. The debris lay to the right of the road, the empty homes, some burned to the ground, to the left. If he stared at the lahar long enough, he imagined it moved, glacially, like a giant, sated, scaly snake.

"That's called a lahar," he said over the wind. He wanted to get out of the town center, avoid the predatory squatters and marauders. The people who were just driven to take other people's supplies. And worse, like this murderous tribe with the flour or the white dye on their faces.

They were like the Picts from ancient Scotland, which he had read about once. But these desperadoes with the white faces, that had nothing to do with culture. *Where the fuck did they come from?* he thought.

"What's a lahar? Sounds like 'har har'."

"They are anything but funny. Well, you knew that already. It came out of the volcano."

"No kidding, man. I was here! I saw it! Kapush!" She made a hand motion like an explosion.

"Call me Coop, not man, OK?"

"Kay, Coop..."

"What's *your* name?"

"Ruff."

"Ruff? What kind of name is that?"

"That's what Turk calls me."

"Ok, I get it. What's your real name?"

"Ruff. I *told* you. So what's a la-hair?"

Cooper adjusted his hands on the steering wheel, and for the moment, oh so brief, it felt like the old days, a drive through the country with a sweet little girl who reminded him of his sister.

"You know Mount Rainier is covered with ice and snow? Tons of cubic meters of the stuff. Cubic miles, more

10

like. When the mountain exploded, all this ice and snow melted and came loose and mixed together with rocks and mud. It made a hot slurry, a giant burning wave."

"Slurry?"

"Like oatmeal, but that you would never want to eat..."

He came to an intersection and slowed down, rolled through it. Smashed up, charred carcasses of cars and trucks lay about. The pale sun settled closer and weakly to the edge of trees.

"It becomes a super hot river, several meters thick. Basically, a river of cement; all this stuff congealed together and knocking all the buildings and high-wires down, covering the roads. Well, you can see what it's done."

He glanced at his rear-view mirror; no one following them, along the path of destruction. Flakes of volcanic ash floated like dirty snow. The sky was leaden gray. He knew they were still too close to the base of Mount Rainier to see its summit. He also knew the mountain was still pluming ash and debris, building a cloud that was visible from space.

Where the lahar passed through, the neighborhoods were obliterated; others still stood, with the odd randomness and selectivity of a tornado or wildfire. He passed a few men, shuffling forlornly through still-intact yards and half-destroyed homes, wearing rags and casting dark-eyed, apathetic stares. This was a land where help was not coming. Cooper realized that. He kept driving with care along the pot-holed, debris-littered road. The gas for the Jeep wasn't going to last forever.

"I'm hungry," the girl announced.

"Well, at any moment, we'll be able to dip into a Wendy's, Jack In The Box, KFC, you name it."

"I like Chipotle," she said.

He looked at her with a half smile. "Expensive tastes, huh?"

"You bet. Nothin' but the best."

One of the best things about his remote property in Telluride was that he didn't have to look at any of those strip-mall franchises; he was too far into the wilderness. Now most of them in the Seattle area were in ruins. Maybe that wasn't such a bad thing, he ruminated, feeling subversive and light-headed. Maybe they can all just start clean.

Don't think about fast food, he thought, it's only going to make his stomach feel emptier. The last things he had to eat were crap about a day ago; limp beef jerky and stale pretzels he'd found in a lousy dumpster. Dumpster diving.

"What was the name of your town?"

"I don't remember," she murmured, her head averted toward an untouched stretch of woods sporting fall colors.

"Well, would you recognize your neighborhood?"

"Of course I would!" she erupted. "Do I look blind?"

"Tell me when you see it, will you? I can't read your mind!" I'm going to have to get out the map and read through some towns with her, he thought. This was turning into a wild-goose chase already, which in these parts can be fatal.

He imagined himself back at his cabin in Telluride, fire blazing, Palmyra Peak in the window under starlight. It wasn't utopia–*there are no utopias*–he said to himself; but it's a good home. It's still there, he knew it. He held out hope for a return.

He'd still had to keep his bow and rifle handy there, however. That wasn't only because of bears and mountain lions. Even the Colorado countryside, like his childhood state Vermont, had a dark side; the drug addled and the drug dealing, along with the just plain unstable and ornery.

It took earthquakes, eruptions, and the ensuing economic and political chaos, from California to Seattle, to breach the hornet's nest. Now they're left with only the responsibility to protect yourself and others.

He had far less than a full tank of gas. It was becoming less certain they'd make the West Coast, or at least as far as Orting or Puyallup, in the scavenged Jeep. He switched the headlights on; the girl had fallen asleep, fell over like a rock. It gave him time to think. He'd look for one of those rural homes, abandoned with perhaps a few left-over canned goods and a weedy garden with still edible veggies. Anything right now would do.

Fear settled over him with the darkness; a pitch black seeped into the broken sprawl, then the countryside. He'd seen a sign for Carbonado. The Carbon River was probably contaminated by ash and the lahar. He cut his speed to get better mileage on the empty, unlit road, when he saw a carcass, a road kill, off to the side. He pulled over, out of sight and off the emergency lane.

He parked the Jeep in the rough grass and dirt, then he removed the flashlight and his Swiss Army knife from the rucksack. He'd draped a coat over the girl, who was deep asleep.

"Want to come with?" he said to Turk, who climbed out of the backseat and carefully hopped down to the ground. He walked beside Cooper to the roadkill and sniffed it, strenuously, up and down. He licked it a few times. The carcass turned out to be a buck deer, its eyes pried open and mouth sadly spilling blood. Not too much time had passed since it was hit.

He figured it was still edible, if hard work to butcher. "I guess it's our lucky day, eh Turk?" The dog looked up at him, an intelligent animal, he thought. He suddenly realized, out of range of the distracting girl, that he *really* liked having the dog there.

They still had to find a place to slaughter the buck and cook the meat over a fire. He had matches, but the choices of safe spots were limited. He'd make a fire in a clearing about 30 yards into the woods. Turk would warn him of any intruders; you could see vehicles coming from miles away.

CHAPTER 4

He and the dog sat by the fire as embers swirled into the night sky. The shadows leapt in the trees, only the crackle and lick of flames breaking the silence. He'd used the branches of a dead birch tree for fuel. Two hind quarters from the carcass sizzled in the flames, the fat on them bubbling and spitting. He'd carried the girl, who was still sound asleep, coat and all, and set her down by the fire.

It had all taken too long, making the fire and sawing off the dead animal's portions. He'd even dug into the viscera, just beginning to smell, for the liver, and placed that into the glowing coals. Food-wise, he wasn't going to take anything for granted.

He consigned himself to staying there for the night. It was quiet, the Jeep parked in the darkness and making metallic pinging tones.

He noticed the dog drooling. He would sniff at the meat in the fire, then back off from the heat and flame.

"Okay, Okay," Cooper said, fetching his improvised

14

fire tool or spatula, which was a crow-bar he'd found in the Jeep. He speared the game meat and moved it carefully onto a couple of rocks he'd laid in a leafy clearing. Using the knife, he sliced off portions for himself, then gave the leg to Turk, who pawed at the hot meat and fat. Then the dog settled down and began gnawing on the meat-covered bone, holding it between two paws.

Cooper let the meat cool for a minute, then silently chewed on a delicious piece of cooked fat. That was where the calories were, he idly thought. Keep pumping up the calories. A dead deer was actually a great find, he thought in retrospect, enjoying his meal. He put one of the pieces down on a rock and cut it into bite-sized ones, just as the girl began to stir. She woke up and, startled in the fiery darkness, began to whimper.

"Sh-sh. I've got some food for you. It's a campfire. You're okay..."

She came over and huddled up against him.

"Where *are* we?"

"The woods. Just off the road, for tonight."

"This is *scary*."

"We're safe. Turk is right there. Turk likes it here. Don't you boy?" The dog looked up from his food, licked his chops, then pooch-smiled around a pant.

"See? Turk is happy. Dinner is delicious, right Turk? Take some." He handed her a piece he'd cut up. She looked at it skeptically, as if it had to be unsavory.

"Where'd you get this?"

"That five-star restaurant we passed on the road."

"My mom used to make me lasagna. It was my favorite." A piece of burned wood toppled over and sent up a clod of embers.

"You mean Millie?"

She didn't say anything for a moment. "Okay, I'll eat it," she said resignedly. He thought maybe he'd move them into the Jeep, when the fire died down.

He let the dog work on the second cooked hind leg, after he'd cut some more meat and fat off of it. Turk nosed and

15

licked it, then settled down on his tummy and gnawed on the gristly, red-stained bone with the side of his jaws. Cooper had also settled the liver into the fire. It was black on the outside, and red like rare beef within. He sliced it into small pieces, but she scowled at the liver, while chewing on the piece of dark meat he'd coaxed her to eat.

The hind leg made Cooper think of a roast; he thought of Alexis's cooking, the willowy brunette girl who happened to love meat. She had mostly vegetarian friends. She cooked stews and roasts in his cabin and they drank red wine together. That was a few months ago. Alexis was a teacher and a waitress in nearby Ouray, Colorado. The affair was over with for now; he'd really fucked up that relationship. He'd screwed it up in a way that made him think he was going to be a loner forever.

The guy who snow-plowed his road had called her "a catch and a real primo gal–a keeper," and maybe some less choice words when Cooper wasn't around. Before they'd met in an Ouray breakfast place and she started coming over, she was the only thing his Telluride cabin, life itself, was missing; but he didn't know that until he figured he'd lost her.

He fooled around with a stick in the fire, staring into it quietly. He needed some sleep. *What if Rainier blew again big time, during the night...?* Right now, its crater sizzled and smoked like a huge version of his campfire. He'd always keep the keys handy; ready to go.

Something about Alexis's growing devotion to him, had disrupted the predictable rhythms of his cowboy-loner life, and in that way set himself against her. Against them being together. *Stupid!* he thought. *You idiot!* She was gorgeous, and kind to him, if a little inscrutable and moody. The first thing he was going to do when he got back to Colorado was look for her.

He was proud, for now, of his food-gathering efforts. Their survival. He ate chunks of the liver, and it made him full and weary. The woods had a piney, cooked-fat odor as the fire began to die down. Everyone seemed comfortable by the glowing coals; he wouldn't rouse them until sunrise. A better plan.

A gratifying sense of order and safety settled over him, the first since Rainier exploded and the lahars went on their rampage. But he knew it was a brittle mood and sensation; disorder would reign once more when the sun came up. Turk lay down by the fire's flickering light, where the girl's eyes shone as she looked out into the night.

"Tell me a story."

"About what?"

"My mom always told me a story before I went to sleep."

*Her mom again...*Cooper thought.

"What about the one about the rabbit in the garden?"

"That will do," she said, from under the coat, after a pause.

He told her a cute story, as cute as he could make it anyhow, about a rabbit that Alexis had been feeding in his garden.

"What else? Is that all?" she said, when it had reached its brief conclusion.

"You mean there has to be more?"

"That was a short story. Too short!"

"But it was a true one, and the rabbit, and the lady, they're still there." Thinking about Alexis, he pictured her beautiful face, glittering green eyes and the way she tossed her long black hair to the side of her shoulders with a fey smile. The vision made him warm, he wanted to go to sleep.

"My dad used to have me recite the Lord's Prayer when I went to bed," he said. "Why don't we do that? Do you know the Lord's Prayer?"

"Of course I don't...know the Lord's Prayer," she said huffily, as her voice trailed off.

He lay down on his back and looked up at the stars. "Repeat after me; Our Father who art in heaven..."

She hesitated, then repeated the poem after him. He remembered most of it, surprising himself, but forgot the middle parts, which he skipped over, finishing with "deliver us from evil..."

By then she'd fallen asleep.

CHAPTER 5

He heard a chorus of crickets, then a distant commotion. The dog roused himself, claws clattering on stiff dirt, then he half barked with a puffing out of his cheeks. The sun crested the trees, white smoke wisped away from the burned logs. The girl was gone; the coat remained.

"Where's the girl?" the comment aimed at Turk, who stood frozen with his nose in the air.

"Ruff, where are you?" he said in a loud hoarse whisper, pulling a sweatshirt back on over his head. He scrambled foggily to his feet. He walked onto the rough path they'd taken through the trees to the Jeep, when he heard voices again.

"I don't *know*," he heard the girl say testily. Then a man's deep voice, the words not made out, but unfriendly, authoritarian. He returned quickly and fetched his bow. "Sh-sh," he said to the dog. "Stay behind me."

He saw a policeman's blue lights pulsating harshly through the bush. When he closed on it, he saw the white and black vehicle parked at an angle with the passenger door open. Two policemen stood looking over the girl, both with sidearms.

Both of them had half beards, were hatless, and wore slept-in, creased uniforms. Cooper thought there was definitely something fishy.

"Where's your dad? Nearby here?" one of them said. "We just have to talk to your dad, now tell me sweetheart..."

"He's not my dad...and he doesn't want to talk to you anyways!"

"We're not getting anywhere with this one," said the man's partner. "I'm puttin' her in the back. Why don't you look around some more."

Then he grabbed her arm, and she screamed and said "Let go of me!"

"Shut up you little brat!"

"You better do as she says," Cooper said, stepping out of the bush, aiming the crossbow at the uniformed man who gripped her arm. He seemed unsurprised by Cooper.

"So here's daddy huh? We're both officers, so you can lower that weapon."

"Something doesn't smell right. Unbuckle your handgun and drop it on the ground."

"What?"

"Drop the gun on the ground."

"You know you'll go to prison for this, or worse," said the other "officer," tensed and to the side. "You only have one arrow loaded."

"At this distance, the arrow will pass completely through his body. You, drop the gun and kick it over to me. You too." The girl walked over and stood next to Turk with her arm draped over him.

"Do it!" she yelled.

"Hush quiet," Cooper said. Then he took a step forward and aimed the arrow at the head of the man who stood nearest the cruiser. "I'll pin your head to the hood of that car if you don't drop the gun belt, now!"

The man unbuckled the belt, dropped it, then used his black boot to nudge it slowly toward Cooper. "Ruff, go pick up the gun and bring it to me."

"Yes sir!" she said, with a willing-to-help chirpiness.

"We're officers you know," the first man repeated, unconvincingly. He fiddled with his gun belt, let it drop to the ground. "We've got backups coming."

"Maybe you once were, and did..." Cooper said.

"I found my brother back there," the man said. "Dead, somebody killed him, looked like with a projectile, a bow."

You mean the low-life back there? Cooper thought. *You share his genes?* The girl brought one gun to Cooper, then the other.

"That's murder," the man said. "When we find the criminal that did it, there's going to be justice served."

"What's your jurisdiction?" Cooper said. "Or once was, before you went rogue."

"Orting," the second officer said.

The girl carefully backed off behind Cooper. He was wary the second guy still might want to make a move on him.

"I want you both on your stomachs now."

"Fuck you," the man closest to him said. Cooper backed off about 20 feet, which the first guy could still cover fast, if he was going to be rushed.

Then the man added, "You don't even know if those revolvers are loaded; you wouldn't know how to take the safety off. And you're down to one arrow..."

"Actually I'll have to rearm," Cooper said, and fired an arrow that plunged into the man's right leg just above the knee. He screamed and his wound blossomed dark red; he collapsed into the dirt, holding his leg on the gravel beside the black-and-white, and howling at Cooper.

"You're going to regret that," his partner said, with a menacing stare. Cooper and the girl had backed off another 20 feet, removing the man's advantage as he reloaded the bow.

"Now down on your stomach," Cooper said. "Or I might do *your* left leg. I might miss and hit somewhere more

21

sensitive." The man went down on his stomach, and Cooper went around to the driver's side of the police sedan. He checked the gas tank; it was three-quarters full. He told the girl to go with the dog back into the woods, where they slept.

Then he told the rogue cop to grab his wounded friend, who lay moaning, with only the back of the arrow protruding from a nasty, bloody hole in his thigh. "Get in the Jeep. Close the door."

He picked up a leather holster at his feet and removed the handgun, which was a Beretta nine millimeter. He switched the safety off. The sky was still gray, the road empty; he felt hollow. "In the Jeep, go." The man opened the passenger door and dragged his wounded friend in, the feet banging over the metal transom and the man howling in pain, then he slammed the door behind them.

"Lock it," Cooper said. He heard the synchronized clicks.

"What are you going to do? The rest of the force knows where we are. That's our squad car. You're gonna get shot, or put away for life."

Glancing at the woods first, Cooper quipped, "I like your vehicle better." He then shot all four of the Jeep's tires out with the Beretta. "The gas tank's fuller, for one."

Then he called out for Turk and the girl. After a minute they emerged from the woods. He urged Turk to jump into the backseat of the squad car, he and the girl took the front. He switched off the rotating blue lights, and they accelerated out of the loose gravel and onto the highway.

CHAPTER 6

"Phew, that was close!" the girl said excitedly, as if they'd just disembarked from a wild roller coaster.

He had two service revolvers now, he reasoned, and that was a good thing. The guns lay on the floor beneath the girl. They were also driving at top speed in a stolen squad car, and that probably *wasn't* a good thing.

"Wilkeson...Burnett?" He named the towns they passed. "Anything ring a bell?"

She shook her head.

"Did your parents live in Orting...Tacoma?"

"No."

Turk started to shift his feet around in the backseat, then he barked once at the wooded suburbs going by; they looked like they had been carpet bombed.

"I think both me and Turk have to make a visit to the woods. What about you?"

"What?"

"Do you have to take a pee?"

"Maybe. When are we going to have breakfast? Do you think that man back there is dead?"

"I don't know, and no."

He'd thought of turning and heading east again–they'll never find this kid's parents at this pace–but the thought of heading back into Rogue Cop Land made him think twice. He pulled the squad car over and parked in some trees. The lahar had passed only about 100 yards to their north; he could see the tangle of wreckage and debris through remaining trees: skeletal piles of twisted metal, uprooted trunks, and crushed homes, all pulverized into an amalgam the color of dead skin. It smelled like a moldy grave.

He stood by a tree and relieved himself as Turk and the girl wandered nearby.

"Don't go far; only where I can see you."

"I'm not going to do it in front of you!" she yelled back with prudish disgust.

He saw her wander down a little draw and behind some trees, with Turk in tow. Then he zipped up his pants and followed them.

It looked like the earth had spit up bile to ooze across the countryside; in fact, that's close to what had happened, as good a characterization as any. The lahar filled the narrow valley, beginning at what was left of a riverbank, on their side.

The calamity wasn't the fault of humans this time, or man-made. Their sin was complacency.

The sky was quiet, bird-less. They'd all fled the Rainier region, leaving an eerie silence in their wake.

Fifteen days ago, Cooper had been asked to help guide a big climb on 14,410 ft. Mount Rainier. He'd jumped at the opportunity. Great pay for only four days, roped to clients, mostly high-wage earners from L.A. and Seattle, looking for adventure and bragging rights. The outfit had paid for his flight, Denver to Seattle, then they'd picked him up in a van and drove to Mount Rainier National Park.

They started the climb the next day and spent the night at Muir Camp at 10,000 feet, then they were up cooking

24

breakfast for the climbers in the mess tent, when all hell broke loose. Tremors shook the mountain, sending avalanches down all four flanks of the no-longer dormant volcano. One of them wiped out the tents at Camp Muir, sparing only a small wooden shelter and the mess tent. When it became obvious that an organized rescue was impossible during an eruption, Cooper fled. It was every man for himself.

He left injured guides and clients behind which made him guilt-ridden, but there wasn't enough time for either transporting bodies on sleds or helicopter evacuations. He sat on his rucksack and rode it downslope most of the way to the lodge at the trailhead, just as columns of super-heated, high-pressure gases shot from Rainier's frozen summit, melting tons of ice, snow, and permafrost, and forming the first of many lahars.

He hitched a ride in a van that drove 70 mph down a mountain road that was designed for 40. It felt like the end of the world, with ash and smoke blocking the sun, and panicked, desperate people fleeing in all directions; the first major full-on eruption hadn't even happened yet. If it had, he would have been vaporized on his way down Rainier.

Although he didn't know it at the time, a lahar was coming up behind them at 50 mph, covering in hot sludge and incinerating everything in its 400 yard-wide path. This event was the "big one" they'd been warned about in the Seattle-Tacoma metro area for decades, so much so that few people cared or pondered it anymore.

When the van ran into gridlock on the highway between Mount Rainier National Park and the big cities, Cooper had leapt from the vehicle and ran to higher ground. That's what had saved his life; no one in the van had followed.

When he topped a ridge by the highway, after going all out non-stop, he watched the white-hot lahar approach, boiling furiously and huge and implacable, making a tremendous roar. It plowed into the traffic; cars, trucks, and buses seized, toppled, riding the roiled lahar surface like so much flotsam and jetsam in a flood, until they blew up or were consumed, wiping out hundreds of people.

Like giant, apocalyptic fingers, multiple lahars jetted down Rainier's flanks and all the surrounding valleys, east and west, destroying towns, utilities, buildings, dams, poisoning water supplies and submerging rivers, knocking out airports, military or otherwise (aircraft couldn't fly through the dense ash anyways).

It was midnight at noon. He wandered the blasted landscape for days until he found any green vegetation, or anything more to eat. Civility lasted about that long; help was not going to arrive. It was Katrina, times about 100. Similar devastation, although he didn't know it at the time, was taking place in California along its various fault-lines.

Food supplies were quickly exhausted. Desperate stragglers wandered the countryside, looking for anything to eat. Shane shifted into raw survival mode.

The sky was empty, ashen; once, the clouds rained black, the gritty puddles running the color of ink. A few people drove on the roads not already smothered in cement-like goo, using only the gas left in their tanks.

They hadn't seen the last of Rainier's massive upheavals, and even he realized that. He'd spent a few days that were like the calm before the storm.

He wandered down the draw and found the girl standing with Turk, seated loyally next to her by a tree. They watched something, across the lahar, which had partially dried and allowed a creek to form from what had once been a river. It was a deer, a doe, with two fawns, drinking from the creek. She saw him watching; the deer dipped their heads into the water then looked back up, twitched their ears, shy and alert.

"Please don't kill them!" she said after a pause. "They didn't do anything to us! They're just trying to get a drink. They're so innocent...don't kill them!"

"I won't," he said, along with a sinking feeling that it would be a while before they saw any game, any at all. "We might get some water though." They watched until the deer turned away from the stream, made their boney-legged way back up the riverbank, and disappeared into the woods.

They had time to get water and filter it. They would be taking a risk, Cooper thought, as the water could be contaminated. He only had a filter and tablets that would kill bacteria or parasites like giardia–he was afraid heavy metals like arsenic and cyanide, from the lahar, had contaminated the stream. But they had no other options–they had to drink. They could go several days, at least *he* could, without a big meal. But water was different.

They went down to the lahar to where river water was still making its way along the sides of what looked like another gray, lumpy cement waterway. The running water was clear (never a guarantee of safety). He dipped the palm of his hand into the cold water to taste it, then he filled the container from his rucksack that contained the filter.

He added a disinfectant tablet. He filled the liter bottle and they all drank from it, Turk lapping the water from the palm of his hand. Then he repeated the process; it was enough to prevent severe dehydration, but nothing more. After three liters they wandered back to the car; it was nearly noon and they were about five miles outside of Orting, Washington, or what was left of it.

CHAPTER 7

He drove with the window down; pale, warm sunlight leaked through the clouds. For once the wind smelled clean, swept of dust. He thought it must be coming from the water, Puget Sound.

They passed a few people on the road, refugees like themselves. Sometimes the dejected people waved, thinking that Cooper was a real policeman. He'd opened the girl's window; she looked thoughtfully outside and let the wind blow through her hair. He wondered if he'd ever have a daughter, if he'd get back with Alexis, marry, have kids.

She looked over at him. "You have muscles," the girl said. He laughed. She reached over and touched his bicep, a balled up muscle, and his forearm, which was like a steel worker's or a ballplayer's.

"I do a little climbing. Work with the axe. Your arms get like that."

"Like Superman." She sighed. "I'm hungry."

He looked in the rear-view mirror and the dog was

panting heavily, looking out one window and then the other. He recalled Turk's look when they watched the deer, almost seeking Cooper's permission to chase them.

"That's what we're going to do next, look for food."

They hadn't driven much longer, just when he was getting his hopes up they might reach the coast, when the cooled lahar's path swung in a southerly direction and covered up the road. He slowed and braked the squad car in front of the looming obstacle. It looked like a hardened sculpture designed to depict abject catastrophe.

The front ends of vehicles stuck up out of it, a gasoline truck's trailer with the tires dripping with brown, dried glop; a human arm and leg. They couldn't go any farther. The sun was going down. He looked over his shoulder and he could see the monumental cloud billowing from Rainier's summit, like another mountain growing off the top of it.

He could turn east again, but they'd just run out of gas, confront further eruptions, and be back to square one. If they survived it.

"What do we do now is start walking guys. There's a town up ahead."

The girl started crying. Tears flowed down her cheeks and she sobbed heavily. "I want Millie and Tom," she cried mournfully. "I'm hungry!"

He got out of the squad car, opened the passenger door behind him, and removed the rucksack. He strapped it on. He called for Turk, who stepped down carefully onto the road. Then he went around to the other side and opened the girl's door; she sat inside pouting, wiping her tears with the back of her hand.

"C'mon, we can't stay here."

"Why?"

"Because this is where the road stops."

She looked around the darkening, broken barrens that stretched in all directions from the car.

"There's *nothing* out there, but cold, and night, and mean, terrible men, and monsters!" She looked at him with wet eyes and a beseeching expression that broke his heart.

"Here, that's okay." He held out his hand and she gripped it. He pulled her gently out of the car, she wrapped her arms around his neck and buried her face in his shoulder. He picked her up by her legs and hugged her to his chest.

"We'll find your parents. It'll be soon, sooner than you think." In the back of his mind he thought there would be refugee centers closer to Tacoma and Seattle. If luck would have it, they'd run into her father and mother.

He carried her away from the car. He already had a rucksack on his back with about 30 pounds of stuff, including his crossbow, knife, matches, a flint, a few layers, and a medical kit, but this was the way it would have to be from now on.

He called for Turk, who sniffed warily at the monstrous presence of the lahar. It stunk to high heaven, like the inside of a sewage tank, filled with wet mud. Reluctantly, they walked slowly towards some woods about 50 yards away across an empty field, as dusk gathered.

CHAPTER 8

When night fell, they saw a pool of light through the woods. It wavered amidst the impenetrable darkness, the charred air. He figured it was either a bonfire or possibly a house. Everything was silent but an audible, metrical knocking, like iron on wood.

They walked toward the light. When they got closer, Cooper put the girl down then said, "You stay here with Turk. I have to check this out; make sure it's safe. Maybe they have food. I'll be right back. Just pet Turk, right boy?"

Turk sat down, licked his chops eagerly, as though anticipating a movement toward better tidings, rather than this fruitless march through the dark forest.

"That'a boy," he said.

The girl squatted down beside the dog and put her arm around him. He left the rucksack with the other two, including a flashlight. He unsheathed the knife and gripped it tight and crept toward the wavering light. He could hear the ponderous sound of his boots on dry leaves and twigs. As he got closer, he saw the shimmer and lick of flames; it was a tall fire. No one seemed around. The knocking of metal on wood had stopped.

Still clutching the knife, he crept closer until he stood behind a thick tree. He saw the shell of an enclosure, with the outer walls burned away. The structure contained a stone fireplace, in which the fire roared. The stump of a tree sat off to the side, with an axe embedded in it. All he could hear was the crackling flame; he decided to scout out the periphery, after standing stock still to detect any sign of movement.

He moved away from the tree and took about four steps, when a booted leg flew out and smashed the hand containing the knife, which tumbled into the pine needles. Seconds later, he took a tremendous hit from behind. The force of the blow threw him onto the hard ground; this muscular person, he was nearly overwhelmed, had legs tightly wrapped around his waste and had got him in a choke hold.

"Don't move, or I'll snap your neck." He was shocked to hear a female voice close to his ear.

"Let go...I mean no harm," he choked out in a muffled voice as they writhed on the ground. "Really!"

She had him completely immobilized. It felt like she could rip his head off. But after the longest minute the hold relaxed. He rolled away to catch his breath.

"What the *fuck*?"

"What are you doing here?" she demanded. She leapt to her feet and stood in the shadows, a compact lady with thick muscular legs, wearing a ski cap.

"I'm with a small girl," he grunted. Leaning on an elbow, he ran his hand over his disheveled hair, then looked at it, searching for blood. He was sore in different spots. "We're looking for food."

"Where is she?"

"If I can get up, we'll go get her."

"What were you doing with that knife? Why were you sneaking up on me?"

"As a precaution. Things aren't so safe around here, in case you haven't noticed." He stood on his feet unsteadily and yelled out for Turk. Twice, then he heard a bark and commotion off in the woods.

"Mind if I go?" he said.

"I'll follow." She had his knife in her hand.

"Over here!" he yelled out as they walked back into the woods. The flashlight appeared and they saw the circle of light, bobbing around.

"You living in that house?" he said.

"I've been squatting there a bit."

They reached the girl, who shined the flashlight in their eyes. She handed it to Cooper; Turk padded over and sniffed the woman, who reached out and scratched his neck. She seemed to relax, having seen that there was more to Cooper than the grubby looking, knife-wielding stranger creeping through the forest.

"Who's that?" the girl said, pointing directly at his former assailant. Cooper shrugged.

"Mikaela," the woman said. "What's your name?"

"Ruff."

Mikaela laughed. They were walking back to the burnt-out house and the fire.

"That's a funny name."

"She got her name from the dog, Turk," Cooper said.

"We stole a police car," the girl said, proudly.

"That's exciting." Then she looked at Cooper, who shrugged again.

"We ran into a couple of bad cops. By the way, where'd you learn to take down a man like that?" At the same moment he thought, *good thing you didn't decide to cold cock me with the axe first.*

"I was a MMA fighter. It comes with the trade."

"No kidding? I guess I'm not surprised; it was a first-round knock-out with me. Are you alone?"

"Yes. We should get the fire going again." The flames had died down a bit. They settled down on two fallen trees beside the smoldering embers.

"Where did you come from?" she asked, throwing a

33

few more wood pieces into the fire. The girl stood close to the rising flame, holding her hands out, transfixed.

"The debris blocked the road, about three miles from here. We left the car."

"I'm starved," the girl intoned, her little eyes blinking behind the wavering flames.

"I've got some junk food. Scavenged it from a 7 Eleven in town. Cans of spaghetti, and stuff. I'll cook up some more. Is this your daughter?"

"No. I found her on the road, with the dog."

"I'm looking for Millie and Tom," she chirped.

"Wow, you were lucky, to find this man."

"The other man she was with wasn't so," he said in a voice the girl couldn't hear.

"It's crazy out there," Mikaela said. "A lot of vicious *manimals* roaming about. I thought of not making a fire, on account of the attention, but I got cold, and lonely."

Mikaela had strong features, a small sharp nose, dark hair tucked beneath the cap, tight over her ears. She reminded Cooper of a female rapper he'd seen perform once in Portland, Oregon; a girl singer with a black wool cap pulled down tight. Sinewy dance moves, a daring voice.

"Do you have a vehicle?" he asked.

"No, I'm walking."

"I have guns, by the way. Two handguns, a little ammo. Might come in handy." He sensed she didn't mind; she had already displayed a practicality about violence. He could still feel it in his sore shoulder.

"Wow, really? Let me see one."

Having put the backpack on his shoulders, he placed it down again and removed one of the pistols. He handed it to her. She admired it for a moment, turning it over in her hands. She held it up and sighted it, clipped the safety switch on and off, then briskly unsnapped and snapped the magazine back into the weapon.

"Impressive," she said, as though inspecting a purebred horse. *Wow this one's a firebrand* he thought. Knows her

34

way around guns.

"You can hang on to that," he said, already trusting her.

Turk lay down and put his head on his paws by the fire, which made loud cracks in the silent woods. All Cooper could see was thick darkness around him; a weariness set in. The long day. Mikaela stood up and tossed on more wood pieces in bursts of sparks. The little girl clapped for them.

"How long have you been here?" Cooper asked.

"Three days. There's a town about a mile from here. Still intact, not burned, but ransacked. I found some food–lucky me. I'm just trying to get my bearings, stock up on supplies, before I move on."

"Seen any Army? Any other troops?"

"Nah, you kidding me?" Then she looked at the little girl, who was occupied with the box of scavenged food Mikaela had set off to the side; inspecting cans and bags of things. She was out of range of their voices.

"The other side of the coin," she whispered. "When I was out on the road, I saw a dangerous bunch, I hid from them in the woods. Some kind of bogus militia; camouflage cowboy hats and black bandannas. They had a captive in chains inside of a cart they were dragging. Can you believe that? In this day and age? They were taking him along the road, somewhere. Poor devil. No, you're the first good guy I've encountered."

Cooper wished he hadn't heard that. He'd thought maybe they would encounter kindred spirits from now on.

"I think we'll sleep here."

"Good."

She went over and she and the girl selected a few cans, which they took to the fire. Cooper used his Swiss Army knife, which Mikaela had returned. He pried open the tops, Spaghetti O's and Campbell's Beef Vegetable and pea soups. They removed the paper labels and settled them into hot spots in the fire and quietly watched them cook. Mikaela had a partially moldy loaf of white bread, which they used to mop up the sauce when the soup was done.

35

It was only the type of scrounged food that he would have eaten during penniless college days. Beggars couldn't be choosers, though. Cooper found it delicious.

He poured out some of the soup into an empty can that he'd cut and reconfigured into a crude bowl. He blew on it to cool it off, then set it in front of Turk, who lapped the soup up ravenously. It seemed like he needed a gallon of it. After they ate every last drop of the soup and cheap pasta, they curled up on beds of pine needles and pulled coats and blankets over their heads.

Cooper kept his pistol and bow next to him, using his backpack as a pillow. Last he checked, the little girl slept partially on top of Turk; cuddled up to him. He knew that because she'd stopped talking. He watched the comforting rise and fall of the dog's furred body.

"Thanks for the grub," he said to Mikaela. He wanted to add *and for not killing me back there.*

"My pleasure," she said, then she pulled the blanket over her own head. "It's good to have some company."

They passed out next to the ebbing flames and glowing embers.

CHAPTER 9

The next morning, they ate the left-over soup and spaghetti, then headed back to the same town where Mikaela had copped her provisions. They thought they'd keep their eye out for an abandoned vehicle that could get them farther away from the mountain. Low gun-metal clouds threatened rain; they drifted ominously over the tree-tops, mixed with a dirty brown haze that seeped from the mushroom cloud capping Rainier.

"How did you end up here?" Cooper asked as they meandered along.

"I was supposed to take a bus to Spokane for an MMA match, meet my boyfriend Larson. He's still there as far as I know, but they cancelled my ride when the mountain blew. I'm standing there at the bus station with my bag, with nowhere to go. Now I just want to get to the coast, as far from Rainier as possible, and maybe get a boat north." All she had for baggage, which she'd tossed over her back, was the athletic bag containing sneakers and a few changes of clothes.

They walked slowly downhill through evenly spaced trees. They could see the two rivers, now dirtied by effluent, flowing on either side of the village of Orting. They followed Turk, who liked to go ahead and seek out the smells. They put him on the leash when they got closer to town.

"How did you get into that fighting game?"

"My energy had to go somewhere–I was either going to become a bad kid like some of my friends, or channel it. I ended up landing in MMA. It keeps me in shape, better than anything."

"You the competitive type? I can tell you're disciplined. I never met a gal who had less fat on her, and who could easily rip my head off." He thought longingly of his old girlfriend Alexis, her willowy figure and midnight black hair laying softly almost to her waist. She couldn't hold her own with Mikaela; they were different breeds altogether.

"I've been in MMA gyms since I was thirteen. It changed my life. It gives me a lift, and it keeps me aloft. As a side effect, it helped me with a difficult step-dad. I vowed I'd never lose a battle to a nasty man, like him."

"You won't," Cooper said.

They were near the edge of where homes and streets began. No one around. The air had a metallic, rusty odor, like an old steel-town smell.

The empty, sullen neighborhoods seemed wiped out by a mutant virus. It didn't feel right to Cooper. He didn't want any more trouble, just food and a clear road to the coast. They came down out of the hills and entered a main suburban drag.

The streets were empty of moving cars and pedestrians; the homes unlit. The only sign of humans was a body, anonymously lying on the sidewalk, as if dropped from the sky.

They had Turk on his leash; they figured he'd bark if anything came up. Cooper took his scope out, detached from the crossbow, and scanned all the way down the drag. He saw nothing but burned, looted stores and shattered glass. Down a side street he spotted a weakly flashing red neon sign. They headed that way, along a sidewalk covered with broken glass, windswept trash, and burn marks, from what looked like exploded Molotov cocktails. In the distance, through the scope, he saw two burnt-car carcasses that had collided, one a police car.

A pregnant silence and emptiness had befallen the town, except way down at the end of the street he saw a man scurry, with more of a rat-like than human aspect, across the intersection. He disappeared.

The place, with its storefront window smashed in, was apparently once a mom-and-pop store that sold cigarettes, lottery tickets, rot-gut booze, and snack food. The register and shelves were ransacked. The girl held on to the dog outside. Cooper stood guard at the door with his pistol, the backpack at his feet, while Mikaela poked around inside. She found some partly frozen and moldy burritos in the back of a freezer, Beef Jerky on a dusty shelf, a stale candy bar, and some bruised apples that had rolled behind the counter. No water or other drinks.

When she went into the back room, the door stuck on something. She looked down and saw a man's comatose body with a huge gash on the back of his head. His trousered legs and shoes were splayed into the room.

"Don't let Turk and Ruff in," she called out. She turned the man's head with the pistol muzzle and felt for a pulse, but he was dead. On the wall, she found a cracked framed portrait of a pleasant looking man and woman, from India or Pakistan she guessed. She stored her meagre harvest in her own gym bag, then went back outside.

She nodded inside. "The owner, or another guy in there, is dead. Didn't get much but lousy old food."

"Oh," he said. A situation had evolved where bodies were no longer earth-shattering news.

"Where now?"

"We're on the outskirts of Orting," he said. "It's not 20 miles to Tacoma and the inland bays. Maybe we can find some transportation there. Otherwise..." He looked around regretfully at the girl and the dog. "We walk."

"This place gives me the creeps. We can't stay out here. We're going to have go into houses to find shelter, and real food and water, then get the hell out of here."

They walked towards the river, which flowed past sluggishly, full of debris and looking ill. They found a few restaurants that were in the same shape; front windows busted in, leaves blowing in the open doors. They took turns going in and giving them a quick search. Mikaela did find a week-old bussed tray with a few scraps of edible food, stale bread and meat on the bone, which she added to the plastic bag that held the scavenged harvest.

She came out and said, "Let's look for a place to eat and hide out for the night."

"Yes...I'll take the dog now, Ruff." The girl handed the leash up to him. She looked thin, gaunt, to him.

"Thanks a lot for looking after him."

"I'm tired," she said. "What is this place? What kind of crazy place is this?"

"It's called Orting."

"I don't like it. All the people are gone. It smells horrible, like diapers."

"How do you know what diapers smell like?"

She looked at him blankly, then looked away. She had an expression of jaded disapproval beyond her years, disapproval of the abandoned homes and littered, broken-down streets.

"When are we stopping? Where the heck are we going, anyways? We're just walking, for the heck of it."

"We're fine. We're headed to the coast, to a boat." He gently took Turk and they started walking.

"Which one? Which boat? A ferry?"

"Yeah, ever been on a ferry?"

"Sure I have!"

"We've got food, a candy bar!" Mikaela said, interrupting, somewhat to Cooper's relief. She took the girl's hand, the pistol held loosely from the other one. They walked up ahead on the sidewalk, under the gray, darkening skies.

Cooper was reminded of photographs of battle-torn areas with soldiers holding the hands of war orphans.

This wasn't so different, he thought. Not even a helicopter, an undamaged car moving at normal speed along the road, a federal occupying force, or even people like them, trying to flee the mountain and make the coast. It was a somber, bad dream.

They entered the first undamaged and intact home they could find, with an unlocked front door. It had a broken screen door hanging off it, a shriveled shrub in a pot. A pile of black ashes stood in the middle of the wooden porch, but the house wasn't burned down. Cooper went in first.

He yelled out, "Hello!" No one answered. He moved quickly through the first floor, including the kitchen, with broken glass on part of the floor and a sink full of dishes. He found the kitchen empty. It smelled like a house was supposed to smell, with no mold, rot, or worse, like it was taken care of but abandoned quickly.

He went up the stairs to the second floor. A family portrait hung on the wall, two young parents with three children seated in front of them in their Sunday best. He hesitated before he went into the bedrooms, dreading what he might find. But they were all empty, one of the kid's rooms with all the drawers pulled out and still a worn pair of pajamas tossed onto the bed.

They'd left in a hurry, but maybe expected to return soon? he wondered. A third flight of stairs led to a closed door; an attic–he yelled up there and no one answered.

Satisfied, he ran back down the stairs and told the others to come in. They gathered in the living room, including the dog. Mikaela pulled out her food. She borrowed Cooper's knife and cut up the burrito and the Snicker's into four even pieces each, but they didn't give any Snicker's to the dog. They sat on the rug and ate quietly; the girl chewed the food slowly with her legs crossed, then she lay out-stretched on the floor.

Mikaela picked her up and carried her upstairs to one of the bedrooms. Cooper chewed on the stale burrito and looked out the cracked front window to the silent street. It wasn't a bad combination with the Snicker's bar. The scrounged food that at the moment tasted wondrous.

He locked the front door from the inside. He heard nothing from upstairs, so he walked up and followed the soft voices. The girl lay in one of the children's beds, clutching two dolls.

"Millie and Tom," she said, when she saw Cooper standing at the entrance to the room. She beamed like it was a revelation.

"Yeah, it seems we've found Millie and Tom," Mikaela said.

"Oh nice."

"They were lost for so long," the girl said, then she placed them on either side of her pillow and hugged them tighter, curling up under a blanket. "I knew I'd find them. I knew it..." She closed her eyes, and fell fast asleep.

Cooper and Mikaela left the room, closing the door behind them.

"I thought Millie and Tom were her parents," Cooper said.

"No, she figures these are her long-lost dolls, which is good enough for me." Mikaela looked at him meaningfully as they stood on the top of the stairs.

"She told me what happened to her parents. They were driving outside of Rainier National Park. They stopped on the side of the road, so Amy, that's her real name, could pick some flowers in a field. Then the lahar came all of a sudden and took the car, leaving Amy in the field. The car had her mom, dad, little brother Joey, and her dolls, Millie and Tom."

CHAPTER 10

He'd fallen asleep in one of the living-room chairs.
Then Turk pawing and scratching at the front door jerked him
awake. Cooper stiffly pulled himself upright out of the chair.
He found the leash. He hooked it onto the dog's collar; then he
located Mikaela in the kitchen. She'd lit a candle and gone
through the refrigerator, which was empty except for spoiled
fruits and a carton of sour milk. Remarkably, however, there
was a little running water left from the faucet; she'd filled a
pan. Her own eyes had a puffy, just-slept look, as she arranged
cups, the pan of water, and remaining food on the table.

"Did you conk out?" Cooper asked, seizing one of the
cups and draining it.

"I did. Amy's out like a light, under the blankets."

"Good. It's better than sleeping outside. I've got to
walk the dog. He's about to poop on the floor."

She gave him a sidelong glance with a half smile. She
looked a lot prettier without the wool cap, her auburn hair
fluffed to around shoulder length. Bright, calm, green eyes.

43

"Sounds positively suburban," she said.

"Yeah, the burbs without the suburbanites."

He picked up the leash, grabbed his crossbow on the way to the door, then both he and Turk went outside.

Turk immediately pulled strenuously on the restraint, plowing his nose into leaves and locating new scents.

The wind blew leaves and clutter along the dark streets, which had the bleak, somnolent atmosphere of a graveyard. He heard nothing but the creak of branches, and what he thought, a low rumble from the horizon. The air had a sour-sweet odor, as if from a pet-food factory; but it had to be the polluted river smells mixing with the ash and fumes from the lahar. It was puke from the center of the earth, he thought, walking the dog halfway down the block.

They kept going and reached an intersection. He let Turk explore a tangle of bushes and trees. He saw a pool of moving lights far at the end of the street, which was laid out straight a mile or more ahead. Could be a car, could be a flashlight, could be a group carrying torches, he thought. He rounded up Turk and they walked around the corner onto another road. The dog pulled hard, like a husky on a sled team.

"C'mon Turk, we can't go forever," he complained. All the other homes were dark and likely uninhabited. Once again, he wondered where everyone had gone.

He heard a loud pop pierce the night, a gunshot. Then two more: pop! Pop! Men shouting, the voices coming from the direction of their house.

Shane called for Turk and they ran together, to the intersection, and then around the corner along the street. More loud pops broke the deep windy silence. From a block away from their sanctuary, he spotted a stocky man in a drab green coat prowling and crouching on the front lawn. He quieted the dog and they hid in some nearby bushes.

The man wore a black kerchief and he had that floury dust on his face. One of the Picts, no doubt. A second man came running up out of the shadows. Both of them clutched weapons, one a handgun, and the other what looked like a grappling hook.

Cooper and the dog knelt together in the shadows, watching. The man with the gun knelt down on the lawn in a firing position. "You're on your own Turk," Cooper whispered, fitting his crossbow with an arrow.

He ran in a crouch across one adjacent yard, then scrambled over a wooden fence, and sprinted to a row of trees. He heard several more shots fired, pops like cherry bombs in succession. He spotted at least three men on the front lawn, including the guy with the grappling hook. Two of them looked pinned down on their stomachs by Mikaela firing the pistol, as pops and flashes came from a second-floor window. The window in front was shattered and gaping open. He knew she'd be almost out of ammunition.

He felt swamped with fear and guilt; he'd left the two girls alone. The man with the hook left his companions and sprinted around the back of the house. He whooped, like a cheap movie depiction of an Apache Native American, as he ran.

One of the remaining attackers rose up to one knee with his arm extended and the handgun aimed through the second-floor window. Cooper already had a fix on him in the scope. He lowered the cross-hairs to just beneath the man's left shoulder, the firing one. The arrow made a twang sound and sliced the air in seconds. It hit home.

"Bull's eye," he whispered, his heart racing. The strike knocked the man over onto his right side; he gripped the arrow impaling his body, kicked his legs spasmodically, then weakly let go of it. Cooper rearmed and headed in a crouched run to the back of the house.

He found the hook man jiggling a latch on the backdoor. He heard Turk barking out front. There was no negotiating with these crazies. They'll kill Mikaela and take Amy. So that was that; no help was coming. It would have already arrived. Before the man could get through the backdoor, Cooper drilled him between the shoulder blades with an arrow. Leaving the body at the backdoor step, he ran

45

back around to the front of the house, his heart beating like a hammer.

When he got there, Mikaela was standing on the front lawn.

She looked at him wild-eyed. She was scared also, he thought, but warily triumphant. "He ran when he saw what you'd done to his buddy, that other one with the Halloween face. The coward, he chickened out."

"You okay?"

"Yeah."

"You sure."

"Yes," she said, breathing heavily and wiping a tear off her cheek.

"Where's Amy?"

"She never left the bedroom."

"That guy is gonna come back with his friends."

"I know. We have to go."

Cooper stood over the dead man as Turk wandered up to the body and nosed its thigh.

He leaned down, put his foot on the dead man's chest, and gripped the arrow by its feathered end. It resisted his pull, then it came out like a dried cork from an old bottle.

They went back inside and found Amy, sitting on her bed with her hands over her ears. Cooper went over and picked her up. Mikaela collected her belongings, including Millie and Tom.

"Shoot, I thought this place was going to be home for a few days," Mikaela muttered bitterly.

"No place is, for very long."

They gathered the rest of their things when they got downstairs, the meagre food and water; blankets. Cooper thought they should go out the back. He rolled the limp, heavy body of the second assailant away from the backdoor frame. He recovered his arrow, then hid the dead man in some shrubs after dragging him by the armpits across the dirt lawn. Then he put on his rucksack, picked up Amy again, and they wandered with Turk back out into the night.

46

They walked for about an hour. They found a worn dog-walking path through the stricken exurb, traversing empty yards and clumps of woods that separated neighborhoods. The backyards were silent, with chain-link fences and soggy volcanic ash floating in the built-in swimming pools. Black ash clouds drifted like a poison tide across a luminous moon.

The wind was cold; a desperation came over him. They had to start searching garages for a vehicle that could get them to the coast, quickly.

They had to stop and put more layers on Amy. At one point they heard high, whooping, juvenile cries coming from about half a mile away. They soon faded into the distance.

They pulled a wool cap over Amy's head and zipped her up into a baggy sweatshirt. They started walking again, sticking to thinned wooded lots beside a street. They came upon a woman wandering down the middle of the road. She acted lost and vague, calling out a man's name, "Danny...Danny dear where are you? Danny?"

CHAPTER 11

They watched the woman shamble along until she was gone around a corner. They stopped in a wooded gully next to a school playground. The plan was to hide out, build a crude windbreak that would get them through the night. They spread out some scavenged blankets around an old tree, then Mikaela and Cooper made a pyramid around the trunk, constructed of broken branches and loose pine bows. Building a nest inside the cone, with every soft thing they could find, the two adults took turns watching out, as the other and the child slept.

The morning light the next day was flat, the rising sun masked by a milky haze. Cooper sat with his legs crossed on the ground. He still gripped the crossbow, as though he would have to use it at any moment. He was a killer now, he'd realized. He thought he was condemned to that label. Yet he was once a man who couldn't shoot an animal for sport.

Silence reigned; it seemed like not a soul existed, not even a bird. The rampaging men hadn't made much of a search for them, he thought idly, but they might today.

He decided to make a small fire. They had a few hot dogs, moldy and hard as a rock when Mikaela found them back in the freezer. They'd thawed out somewhat. He made a bed of dry twigs and grass and some cardboard litter, got it going with the flint, then added bigger sticks on top. The sticks glowed, puffed smoke, and caught; a bigger flame rose and licked in the morning breeze. He put more wood pieces on, there was plenty of it, then speared the hot dogs with other sticks and balanced them over the fire.

He dragged a log to nearby the fire, and sat down on it.

He made cowboy coffee with his camping container. It had a plunger and filter; you put old coffee grounds on the bottom, then poured hot water over that. The coffee seemed an integral cog of survival, like any old morning.

Mikaela stirred and sat up, watching him, her hair flattened on one side. She pulled the cap down over her head. Amy still slept deeply, under a blanket, head on Turk's furry torso. The dog lay still, just his ribs moving slowly up and down.

Mikaela got up from beneath a blanket and sat next to him; he handed her the cup, which she sipped gratefully with both hands. "Quiet night," she said, then she dropped her head onto his shoulder.

The small fire made everything seem calm, unhurried, and safe, which he knew was an illusion that would only last a few moments.

"We made it this far, we're alive," she said softly, relieved for the time. The fire made pleasant crackling noises. Cooper made a washing motion with his hands to warm them up.

A darker shadow fell over them, from Rainier's ash cloud. Mikaela had a distasteful look as she gazed around the deadened neighborhood.

"...Even though the rest of the world seems utterly fucked."

"By the end of today," he said, raising his cup in what

49

he figured was the western direction. "We'll be on the coast. I know it."

"Hope so. Hope that's true, I really do."

"Ever had anything bad happen before," he said, looking back to her. "I mean, really bad. Like this. You're really tough as nails, under fire. It seems like nothing phases you, like you've been through something before."

"It's an act."

"I doubt that."

After a minute she said, "I had a twin, Missy. Missy Brand, my dear sister. She drowned when we were twelve. She went swimming at night in a lake, during a sleep-over." She swallowed a lump in her throat. "She never came back. We all looked for her. All night. Kids and parents standing on a shore under the stars, with blankets on their shoulders. The police, putting a boat in and divers and flashlights everywhere. The sun came up, the divers found her. I cried my eyes out, then I was mad. So *angry,* at her, that she had left me that way. Alone. Without saying anything. No goodbyes. One minute she's stealing my Pepsi and drawing on my arm, the next she's dead. Forever. After doing something, probably dumb, definitely risky.

"It was the forever part that made me so confused, so mad. I couldn't yell at her anymore. I couldn't tell her not to do dumb and risky things, that she was my sister, my twin, and I needed her around. She was only twelve; so...dumb."

She reached over and tapped the fire with a stick, as in lightly beating it in frustration, then she tossed the stick in. "That weekend, I went to the MMA club and started training. Competing. I never stopped."

"Wow."

"What about you?"

He looked away, opened his eyes wide at nothing; the adjoining yards, once active with families, were vacant.

"I lost my dad, when I was seventeen. He flew small planes. He crashed one into a mountain in California. Him too, probably made a dumb mistake; flew at night, in bad weather. He was my hero, he was a risk taker. He took me hunting once, for black bear in Vermont. I was scared shitless, but I thought he could do anything, feared nothing. He shot a bear and dressed it on the floor of the woods, and I knew it was nothing I'd want to do, but he was King of the Mountain.

"We played baseball together, went fishing, he was going to teach me to fly. I remember when my mom told me about the crash, about how he was dead. I couldn't believe it. I was in complete disbelief. I didn't talk for days afterward. The part about him being my dad went by way too fast. Boy, did that change my way of looking at everything."

"I would have liked to know him," Mikaela said. "Knowing you, I can picture what he was like."

Amy watched them silently from her blanket, until she mumbled in a high voice, "Where *are* we?"

Cooper looked at her and smiled, glad to have the subject changed, even though he'd liked telling Mikaela.

"Still in Orting. We getting out of here today though. Do you want something to eat?"

CHAPTER 12

They ate the hot dogs, gathered up everything into the rucksack and gym bag, then moved on. They could rely on Turk's nose as a warning signal, because Cooper knew that they had to stick to a road to get anywhere. The morning had a preternatural stillness, as if the agitated earth was resting but ready to crack open again, releasing its malignant contents.

Cooper had the dog on the leash; Turk led them down the cluttered road. Mikaela carried Cooper's pistol, in her left hand as her arm hung to the side. She walked behind him, her other hand in Amy's, who scrutinized the silent road with her curious eyes. The street headed west, towards Tacoma and the Pacific Coast. That was more than 20 miles away.

Soon, they came upon a woman sitting on a stoop. As she smiled, her eyes, rather than focusing on them, gazed through them and beyond.

"I hear you!" she said. "Friend or foe?"

"Friend," Cooper and Mikaela said, at the same time.

"Where are you headed?" she asked.

"Out of town," he said. "Towards Tacoma."

"I know where we can get a car," she said matter-of-factly.

"Where?" Cooper said. He'd seen her before, the woman walking down the middle of the road. She had cocoa skin, short, dark hair, and a slim body beneath a sweater, which she tugged around her.

"My home."

"Where's that?"

"Daffodil Ave., just after the school. A lavender house, you can't miss it. But you're going to have to show me. Cuz I'm blind."

Cooper looked quickly at Mikaela then said, "Sure, come along."

She stood up, still smiling, and stretched out her hand. He stepped forward and took it.

"Strong!" she said. "And warm...I'm Beatrice. My friends call me Bea."

"I'm Cooper. Shane Cooper. This here's Mikaela Brand."

"How do you do?" Mikaela said, offering her hand, which the lady took in both of her's. "This little girl's Amy."

"My friends call me Ruff," Amy said, reluctantly pushed forward by Mikaela. Beatrice hugged her and called her "dear." An air of recently lost civility hung over the gathering; meeting new people, shaking hands, exchanging greetings. Cooper thought maybe when they reached the coast, things would return somewhat to normal. The coast stood for promises, for events that might or might not happen. They started walking.

"I don't have a street map," Cooper said. "If I found the school, could you lead us to Daffodil?"

"Yes, of course. The school is on the main street. My husband, Danny, I know he's there waiting for me. At home. He must be sick with worry. We have no way to call each other. He wouldn't leave without me. We'll go there, we'll get the car, it's a Subaru, and we'll all go."

53

"There's a dog, too," Mikaela said.

"His name is Turk," Amy said, more eagerly than before.

"Oh how nice," the lady said. "I must pet him." She stopped and put both hands on her knees, with the wide-open, looking-beyond eyes that made them appear visionary. Turk ambled up to her; she clutched him while looking in another direction, and roughly stroked the long fur, from shoulder to back. "He is *so* beautiful, and soft," she said.

"We better go," Cooper said. They went around the corner as a group, back to the main drag. The lady said that if they hadn't passed it already, the school would be close, on the left.

When they reached the long, single-story brick building, they found a wind-swept yard that embodied the invisible presence of children.

The building was empty. The wind clapped a roped fitting against the metal flagpole, with a clanging sound like a lone schooner at sea.

"The first right," Beatrice said. They crossed the street. The sky was dark with clouds and ash, for so close to noon. Flashes could be seen on the horizon east, toward Rainier; small explosions or eruptions. They turned right on the sidewalk down Daffodil Ave.

Beatrice seemed confident in her directions. She walked with a marked grace, short steps, one hand balancing on Turk's back. The dog walked beside her without deviating, as though trained to. Before long, Cooper saw the lavender house; he stopped in front of the mailbox.

"This is 78 Daffodil Ave.," he said.

"We're here," Beatrice said. "Oh Dan! Oh Danny," she called out, her head tipped back. "We're here! It's Bea!"

Cooper noticed that the house seemed quiet with no lights. "Do you know where the car keys are?" he asked.

"I have a copy on me," she said. "But Danny will also have a set with him. He always does. He always has piles of keys to the house and car with him!"

They all walked toward a connected garage on a clapboard house. They opened a door between the garage and the home. To the right, Cooper could see the car parked inside. "Car's still here," he mentioned. Another door opened to a kitchen; the door was unlocked, he held it open for Bea. She called inside again, but still nothing in response. She walked inside the house, through the kitchen, calling for "Danny."

Amy, Mikaela, and Turk came in behind them. Mikaela went into the refrigerator. "Food. There's old pizza in here, and milk, and carrots and mayo." She pulled them out, the pizza partly eaten in a carton, and set them on a table that had three chairs. Cooper walked through the first floor hallway with Beatrice, who continued on, calling out her husband's name, into an office. "I guess he's not home, now..." he heard her fading voice. He turned onto a staircase, to the second floor.

He noticed mud on the stairs, bootprints. He got to the top of the stairs; an overturned chair, a portrait of a ballerina hung askew on the wall. More smeared mud around the floor. "We found lots of food!" he heard Mikaela's voice from below, encouraged by the discovery.

He entered a bedroom. A bed was pushed against the wall with the mattress yanked half off of it. A bureau of drawers was pulled out, rifled. Next to the bed, a man's body lay face down. One arm was flung outwards, as if in the middle of a swim stroke. The man wore blue trousers with the back pockets pulled inside-out. Eyeglasses lay broken and flung to the side.

A small, dark red bloodstain lay near the man's forehead. Cooper walked up to the body and knelt down. He felt along the neck for a pulse, but there was none. The side of the man's face was blue, his right eye stuck open. Shane closed the eye, which shut like it was on a hinged lever. He stood back up. He heard Beatrice coming up the stairs.

"Did you see anything?" she asked, feeling her way to the room's entrance.

"No," he said, coming quickly out of the room. "The

55

bedroom's empty." He stood in the doorway. She brushed past him to enter the room, saying, "I should get some more clothes." He stood aside; she immediately walked to the right, to a closet, and opened the door. She took things down with hangars–she found them by memory–and made a pile in her arms.

"It's funny..." she murmured, paused, then shook her head and kept taking things, until she was done.

"When all this happened, I was across town, doing errands; the supermarket, bank, library. I got stuck over across town, then I finally reached him, and he said he'd come pick me up. He never did. Yet the car is still here. I wonder where Danny could be?" She was still talking when she left the room, and he followed her down the stairs.

They sat down on the kitchen table and feasted on the scraps that Mikaela had found, including a box of stale Wheat Thins, a glass jar of caky, dried-out peanut butter, and the stiff-crusted pizza. It all tasted good, and was quickly consumed. He fed some of it to Turk, who chewed the pizza with an exaggerated, wet, clamping-down of his jaws. Mikaela spooned mayo, spread on nothing else, into her mouth.

"To the hungry, " Mikaela said. "Everything edible is a sumptuous feast."

They quietly stood up; Cooper wanted to leave. They could drive into the dusk.

Beatrice leaned on the kitchen counter tentatively. She shook her head. "This is so unlike Danny. I hope nothing has happened to him."

Cooper was completely torn asunder inside, with guilt and a sense of obligation to this lady who's already demonstrated courage and patience, in terrible circumstances.

He shook his head at Mikaela, frowned. He wondered why he didn't just tell her; he thought she'd collapse, refuse to let them take the car, and thus endanger them all. A debate took place silently, in his mind, but Mikaela could read it on his face. They could take the car to Tacoma, he thought, then he'd drive Beatrice back.

"Why don't we get going, get to Tacoma," he said.

"I suppose..." Beatrice said, then she dug into her pockets and produced a metal loop with a few keys on them. She handed them to Shane.

CHAPTER 13

The car rolled slowly out of the driveway. The vehicle was full; Turk curled up in the cargo area, with the rucksack, gym bag, and a bag of scavenged food. The street was empty, as if it was a mellow afternoon on any Sunday.

The sun fought through a massive debris cloud that drifted toward the sea. Flakes of ash floated lazily in the rearview mirror. Over the roofs of the homes, he could see a thick column of black smoke rise in the distance.

Beatrice sat next to him in the passenger seat. "I can't thank you enough," he said. "For the use of the car."

She'd located a pair of sunglasses and put them on. She gazed out the window, regardless. "You found *me*. I wasn't going to make it home alone."

Then she reminded him. "A middle-aged man, salt-peppery hair, wearing a sweater. If you see him, slow down and I'll call out." She rolled down her window, as if she could pick up his scent.

"Okay." Cooper scanned the street watchfully. Empty

yards, overturned trash barrels, an abandoned car jerked to the side of the road with one wheel left up on a curb.

He could hear Mikaela and Amy playing some kind of a word game in the back, then Amy said, "Put that gun away, okay."

"Not yet, kiddo," Mikaela said, her forehead leaning against her own window placidly. "It's not loaded..." But Cooper knew it was, and that it only contained a few more rounds.

"How long have you lived here?" Cooper asked. They drove through the neighborhood, then accelerated onto the main route out of town.

"Forty years, off and on. I'm a townie," Beatrice said. "I worked in the Sheriff's office for most of my adult life."

"The sheriff's?" His eyebrows raised.

"That's right."

"We've had run-ins with this local gang. Maybe you know about them. In fact, except for you, they're almost the only other people we've seen. A bunch of nut-cases with white make-up. They attacked us...we've seen them assaulting people..."

"I think I know who you're talking about," she said. "We arrested members of that gang. Young hoodlums, no jobs or supervision, just waiting for something like this to happen. The local D.A. would prosecute them, but they'd always come back out on the street, like zombies that won't die.

"They have a ringleader we think. Her name's Gladys. You'd more likely give her a bouquet of flowers or a knitting set than a set of hand-cuffs. But she's a shrewd, conniving woman. She owns a chain of laundromats that were used for money laundering, from cocaine and Oxycontin sales. Looking at her, you wouldn't think...Not that I've seen her picture," She laughed dryly.

"But the local cops just say she's apparently a clever and persuasive criminal. She takes in these local thugs like they're all of her orphaned children. So you say you've had confrontations?"

59

"You could say that, yes. I had to kill a couple of them." She went silent for a minute, a weighty silence that left only the sound of the car's engine as they made their way through town.

He caught her looking at him, with her sunglasses. He imagined the visionary eyes behind them. "My!" she said. Then she turned away. "What's the world coming to? Really."

Cooper looked in his rearview mirror and saw a pickup truck cross the intersection two blocks down. He stepped on it, aiming for the highway, and soon they were on the entrance ramp to Route 162.

Once he got out onto the highway, he steered into the passing lane and put the car up to 60 mph. No one else was on the road, until he saw the dark pickup truck appear again in the rearview mirror. It gained on him a bit, and he floored it.

"Make sure your seat belts are on," he said to the others. He figured he only had fifteen minutes to the Tacoma metro area. He hoped they'd be free of the gang once they hit the coast.

Now the pickup was close enough so that he could see two men in the front seat. Behind them, the cloud from Rainier had blackened; it pulsated with fiery eruptions like lightning strikes from a thunder cloud. The highway in front of him was empty and windblown with debris cartwheeling across the road.

"He's closer," Mikaela said. Both she and Amy were staring out the back window.

"Are they bad men?" Amy asked.

"We don't know them," Cooper said. His own crossbow was in the cargo seat with his rucksack. He shot a glance at the gas gauge; *plenty for now*.

When he looked back to the mirror, he noticed something else. He didn't recognize the amorphous presence gaining speed, at first. It was higher than the highway's roadbed, like a giant shadow, and much wider than the highway. It rose up in the mirror ominously.

"Shit! A lahar!" he screamed, pinning the accelerator to the floor. He watched it in the mirror, a blackish brown churning wave, overtake the pickup, which reared up on its rear axle then flipped over backwards. The lahar was gaining, merely several car lengths behind them.

CHAPTER 14

The lahar rose to a height of almost 30 feet. The pickup behind them had been crushed into a third its size. It bobbed sickeningly on the crest of the flowing slurry, burst into flames, then appeared to be consumed. Shane had seen moving shadows of the two people inside. He had the accelerator of the Subaru floored. Amy cried loudly in the back seat.

"It's another one of those la-hairs! Get us out of here! Go! Please! Go!"

"Everybody hold on!" he yelled, fecklessly, knowing they didn't have any other choice. He could feel the lahar's vibrations in the road as they flew and bounced along. His frantic eyes darted back and forth between the rearview mirror and the eerily empty landscape through the windshield. This land was poised for epic destruction.

It was wooded suburbia, with an oncoming mall, Lowe's and Walmart, on the right. Going up to 80 mph, he was able to put several hundred yards between himself and the lahar, which filled his mirror with a frothing, greenish-black mass casting a dark shadow on the remaining highway.

He could see it hit the adjacent landscape as it devastated Walmart, rolling over the one-story warehouse and the cluttered parking lot like an ocean of molasses over a toy house. Neighborhoods, trees, bridges, overpasses, highway signs, vehicles of all kinds, parking lots; one second they were there, another they weren't. The lahar devoured everything in its path, engorged with the pulverized detritus of human sprawl.

Disordered thoughts raced through his mind: he figured the lahar would fill the valley, so their only option would be to seek higher ground at its periphery. But where was higher ground? He only had minutes, maybe one minute, to make a decision. Just when he had decided that he would attempt to outrun the lahar to the coast, hope that it would lose some momentum by spreading laterally throughout the river valley, Mikaela screamed and pointed across the front seat, "Look! Those horses! Follow *them*!"

To the north, perhaps a mile away, he saw a huge herd of horses stampeding in a cloud of dust into a cleave in the far-off foothills. The hills sat alongside the valley. When they neared this spontaneously formed migration, a natural spectacle that struck them mute, he noticed that they weren't just horses: it was a river of all kinds of animals; cattle, sheep, deer, elk, even dogs, coyotes, and smaller mammals like fox and weasels, all following an incalculable drive. Appealing to an imprecation from the blood.

When Cooper looked up, he could see a giant flock of birds flowing in the same direction, to the north of the valley.

"Follow them Shane, go! After them!" Mikaela screamed, jumping up and down in the back seat. He jerked the speeding vehicle onto the breakdown lane and then rattled across an open field. He made a dirt road and lurched along it at high speed. They bounced along in the dust cloud, watching the animals thunder on galloping hooves just ahead of them, with a motion he'd only seen in cable broadcasts of Alaskan elk migration, or the wildebeests in Tanzania.

Now he drove almost directly north, nearly perpendicular to the oncoming lahar's path. It could overtake them at any moment. He noticed the animals shift in a wave pattern, moving slightly west, toward the coast. He followed.

"What's it doing?" he screamed to the others, over a strange roar, and the galloping hooves. "The lahar! Where is it?"

"It's close! It's spreading out!" Mikaela yelled back. "We're okay...maybe."

"Maybe? For how long? Can we make it! I mean in this direction? Can we?"

"Maybe 30 seconds."

"What!"

"We need to get to higher ground! In 30 seconds!"

"Holy shit!"

The animals poured like flood waters into a shallow pass. The road rose imperceptibly. Cooper dared a look to the right, past Beatrice, who stared with mute, morbid fascination, literally blind to what was happening, outside her window.

He saw the towering putrid mass, bigger than any of the others, carrying smashed debris like so many squashed trinkets. It looked like the sludge coughed up by deep oil wells, but multiplied by a magnitude of millions. It was not 100 yards away. Closing fast.

The giant herd angled west, and he was speeding uphill at greater than 45 mph. Amy screamed; Turk barked relentlessly, driven almost mad by the dreamy grandeur of stampeding animals. The herds didn't seem to notice, or acknowledge, them.

"We've only got 50 yards!" Mikaela screamed, her hand on the passenger door handle, as though she was willing to jump out with Amy and run. The Subaru ground through rocks and sand, skidding into a rising switchback. Heads down, the animals tore up the road just ahead and alongside them. Cooper didn't dare look to his right; but one more switchback and they were in the clear.

64

He watched the upper layers of the lahar roll past, with a dour majesty, like the view of a giant ocean liner leaving its mooring.

He began to breathe again.

CHAPTER 15

He reached a pullover, a kind of overlook. He slammed on his brakes. The lahar flowed beneath them, carrying a plunder of death and destruction, filled with torn-up bits of the landscape they had just driven through.

Cooper put his head on the steering wheel and rested. Black smoke from engine oil and dust from stampeding animals suffused the air, already fetid with the lahar's fumes. The animals dispersed; a portion of the herd, the stragglers, many of the slower moving cattle, hadn't made it. A few horses and sheep loped up the road and around the bend, or stood mutely on the edge of the climbing road, heads down, as if mourning the destruction.

Cooper got out of the car and stood looking at the lahar and the ruined landscape. It had been despoiled by geology and humans were no longer imperial.

The others got out and stood by the side of the road, Amy holding Mikaela's hand. Turk leapt from the car, stared at the animals wandering nearby, and began barking. Beatrice broke the silence.

"Thank you for saving us back there."

Cooper glanced at her then away; he was suddenly exhausted, and hungry. When was the last time he'd had a full night's sleep?

"It was Mikaela's idea, and it turned out to be the right one."

"I'm thirsty!" Amy cried out. "Where're Millie and Tom?"

"We brought them in the car," Mikaela said testily. "Remember?" She took Amy back into the car and came back with some water, too, in a half-gallon jug she'd filled back at the house. They passed it around. The Subaru seemed spent; the fenders were dented and muddied, pinging noises came from its joints, and a slight steam wafted from the hood.

"This road must go somewhere," Mikaela said. "How much gas do you have?"

"We're actually doing pretty well with the gas." They would have to find a new route to the coast. He took a drink and gazed out over the valley, which had now been scoured by at least two Rainier lahars. Smoke rose everywhere he looked, nothing much moved. It looked primeval; the leftover region after an asteroid strike.

The valley wasn't utterly dominated by lahar, however. It hadn't stretched to the valley's complete width. Varied buildings were still standing, some, in the town they had just come from.

Beatrice began to cry softly. She took her sunglasses off, long enough for the hazy sunlight to strike her face. "Poor Dan. He was probably caught in that, this horror. A terrible, terrible thing." She sobbed into her hand.

"That's okay Beatrice!" Amy cried out. "One of those la-hairs killed my family!" Her voice betrayed the matter-of-factness of youth.

"Listen, Beatrice," Cooper said. "I've got to confess. I have something to tell you. I feel bad I didn't tell you before. That's my fault. I found a man on the second floor of your

67

house; in the bedroom. Where you got your clothes. He had passed away."

She turned toward him. "You found Danny?"

"Yeah." She seemed to be looking at the mountains, Mt. Baker and the fuming Rainier, and not his face.

"Well...it's not your fault. But I wish you'd said something before. We were married 30 years. We were soulmates. We were, really." She looked away with her wet cheeks and swallowed. She put her sunglasses back on, composed herself.

"I feel sad, but a strange sort of sad, one that has relief in it, too. That explains why he never contacted me; he must have fallen, in all the stress. Had a heart attack. That's awful news, I've been dreading it, but uncertainty and ignorance is worse, I suppose. I'll go back for him, his remains. The town might still be standing!"

"I doubt that," he said, although he had visual evidence of *some* buildings that were still intact, out off the highway, which hadn't been completely buried. At least not yet.

"Think we should start up the car again?" Mikaela said.

Cooper got into the car and it sputtered to life, a rattling coming from under the hood. Civilization, he assumed, lived on the other side of these foothills. It was wishful thinking, but he thought that because they had endured this long, that good fortune must lie around the next corner.

They all got in, and the car pulled back onto the dirt road, which seemed designed for utility vehicles. It offered no guarantees that it would connect them to the coast.

As they rolled slowly up a moderate hill, animals impassively parted. Deer scattered up the hillsides, limping through rocks on boney legs; cows lingered on the precarious roadside, vacuously nodding their heads. Cooper could see herds of black and brown horses reconstituting themselves. They ran together along a border of trees below.

He was half tempted to use his crossbow on one of the deer or sheep for food, but he couldn't get himself to do it. He felt a strong kinship with the animals, and a kind of gratefulness.

The road headed down into a draw that was mostly woods. He saw an excavation like a large quarry, and a half-baked wooden structure that contained a pile of sand. He vowed to take the first road heading west. The sun was beginning to set. He longed for an unobstructed view of the sea.

In the distance, he spotted the beginnings of a suburb, neighborhoods and parking lots, perhaps 20 miles away. From the back seat he heard, "The gals, and the canine, have to make a visit to Mother Nature."

"Haven't we had enough of Mother Nature for one day?"

He pulled the Subaru over to the side of the dirt road. Mikaela, Amy, and Turk clambered out. Turk immediately lifted his leg on a rock, then stood at attention, his nose in the air and ears twitching. Cooper figured it was the herds of animals he smelled.

Beatrice chose to stay in the car. She'd settled into a graceful sadness; he didn't feel the stab of blame. Amy began to run across a field toward some trees, with Turk in pursuit. Mikaela cried out, "Don't go far! Slow down!" It reminded Cooper, who was following them, clutching his crossbow, of when he first saw Amy, standing in the flowers calling for Turk.

He walked across the field behind Mikaela. It felt good, safer, to be on the other side of the hillsides from the lahar, which was like an ever-present malignancy.

"Tell me about this boyfriend of yours. What's his name?" He had a half-crushed candy bar, a Charleston Chew, from the mom-and-pop shop back in Orting. He tore off a piece and handed it to her.

"Shakir Richards."

"Where's he from?"

"Originally, Egypt. His Mom's a Muslim. His father worked for the State Department in Cairo. Then they moved to Spokane. That reminds me..." She pulled a cell phone out of her pocket. Habitually, she attempted to power it up, but of course failed.

"Once I can recharge this thing, I'll try to send him a text. I have no idea where he is now."

"Where did you meet?"

"At the gym. He's into martial arts, too."

"So you kicked and wrestled each other. How romantic." He wanted to kid her. He felt a need to lighten up, draw back the curtain on this darkness that enveloped them.

She half smiled. "Actually, I thought he was funny. And smart." Then they saw Amy and the dog disappear into a dip in the field, toward some trees. Mikaela cupped her hands over her mouth and cried out. "That's far enough Amy!"

Cooper stole a glance at the car; it sat quietly on the empty road.

"Is he religious?"

She looked at him, somewhat warily chewing the candy bar.

"Shakir? Yes, he is. He goes to a mosque, he does his daily prayers, at sun-up and sundown. I've come to respect it. It's a discipline, like mixed martial arts."

"Has he tried to convert you?"

"To Islam?"

"Yeah."

"No. He wouldn't do that. That's not his thing, conversion."

"Do you think he wants to marry you? I've heard a Muslim man can be quite conservative, want to bring up the children as Muslim."

"My, my, you are full of questions today, aren't you?"

"Just curious, you know. Looking for distractions. Sorry if I was pressing too hard. I just want to get us out of here. You know, it's funny. I'm an escapist by nature. Now I truly need to escape. Actually, I'm exhausted. I need to face plant."

"Me too. Before, how did you usually escape? As in life? Getting away."

70

"The mountains, mostly. I'll do a big mountain climb, or a ski. Often alone. It's when I feel most at peace, in the mountains. Sometimes the desert."

"I went to the desert with Shakir once." They stood still in the long grass, keeping Amy in sight. "Utah, outside of Moab. We hiked to the Colorado River as the sun was setting. Pure bliss. I slept in the desert by a fire, in our own campsite. That's what I love about the West, its beauty, wide open spaces. Its remoteness. It fills my spirit, like a sail."

"I couldn't have said it better myself. You're reminding me of Telluride. As soon as we get our butts out of this clusterfuck, I'm inviting you and Shakir to Colorado."

"It's already on the calendar."

He decided to stop while she went on to a copse of trees, where they saw the dog wagging his tail. He found himself jealous of this man named Shakir, who'd he'd never met, but had Mikaela's attention and respect. He couldn't deny it, he and Mikaela had formed a bond, naturally, as they fought for their lives.

When he had gotten most of the way back to the car he heard truck engines from over a knoll. He called out over his shoulder, "Mikaela, stay in the trees with Amy!" Then two pickups appeared coming up each side of the road. They blocked any escape for the car.

CHAPTER 16

They were both Ford F-450s, with men in the back. The men were armed, wearing dark fatigues. There were about four in each truck. He wanted to crouch in the weeds and arm his crossbow, but it wasn't going to do any good. Why now? he cursed to himself.

They pulled over at each side of the Subaru. The men disembarked. Beatrice had opened her passenger door and tentatively stepped onto the roadside. The men approached her, aggressive and unfriendly like.

His instincts told him to run, but that would draw them to Amy, Mikaela, and Turk. When he was spotted, three of the men began to stride towards him, carrying guns. A sickening resignation settled over him. He was afraid they would hurt Beatrice.

"You can drop whatever you've got in your hands there *pard*!" one of the men yelled out. He gently placed the crossbow on the ground. He didn't think they'd seen the others down in the woods.

They got to within about three yards of him and stopped. Over their heads, he could see two of the men, one of them with his hands on Beatrice, leading her to one of the trucks. She cringed and flinched when the man seized her arm.

"You're smart not to run," the one in the middle said. He had a pistol on him, an unshaven face with beefy jowls, and long black greasy hair that didn't fit the fatigues. It was unsoldierly.

"Where'd you guys come from?"

"I'm asking the questions. That your car?"

"No, it's hers. Hey, tell them to take it easy with her, okay?" Cooper said "She's blind. And harmless. She hasn't done anything to you. I'm just giving her a ride to her house. Why don't you let her take the car, and let's all move on out of danger. We have to keep moving."

"Why don't you take your panties out of a twist," he said, and two of the men laughed inanely. "Where are your other pals?"

"Pals? What do you mean by that?"

"What does it sound like, moron?"

The man walked up to him, with his scowling mug not a foot away, and placed the barrel of his gun on his chest. He smelled like Marlboros, no filters; and sourly of bourbon. "The other people that were with you. That's a big car. Got any other companions?"

"Just answer his question," the thug on his left sneered, when there was too long a pause.

The lead desperado shot back at the guy, "Shut the fuck up."

"No, it's only us two," Cooper finally said, backing up a couple of steps. This wasn't going to end well, his gut told him. He needed his Swiss Army knife; he needed to unfold it and jam it into this animal's thorax.

"We're like everybody else," he said evenly. "The lahars took us by surprise. We're lucky to be alive. All we want to do is move onto the next town down there. Find some help."

"*Find some help*," the man muttered, and licked his

lips. "You found it right here. So it's just you riding around with this blind chick. Somehow that doesn't seem right. What are you, her seeing eye dog?"

"The seeing-eye dog!" the other lout slurred vacuously. He seemed juiced-up on something, or juiced down. He carried a crude pike with feathers tied onto the end. A smudge of white paint on his face made his teeth seem blacker.

"Didn't I tell you two to shut your trap?" The man turned and whacked the guy with the pike with the butt of his gun, which deposited the man whimpering to his knees. Then the fearless leader hitched up his pants and grimaced, as though he'd betrayed something, a lack of cool. Then he told the third gangbanger to confiscate Cooper's bow. "And leave the rifle..." he added.

The third man carried a deer rifle similar to the one Cooper had back in Telluride, with a scope. He set it on the ground. Seeing the other man holding his crossbow made Cooper feel more hollow and empty.

"I should just kill you two right now," the man said, impatiently, turning his head to Beatrice, who was now sitting in the back of one of the pickups. "And leave with the car."

"What's the purpose? Of all this," Cooper said. "It's a waste of time, and energy. All of us survivors need to work together." Then he noted how ludicrous it was to appeal to a humanity where none existed.

"We have orders to take you folks back to headquarters," the man said, with a sudden tone shift, as if he represented a calm restoration of order. He pocketed his pistol, picked the rifle off the ground, and aimed it at Cooper, staring through the scope.

"Yeah, you do look familiar," he murmured, moving the scope slightly back and forth, from one of Cooper's eyes to the next. "I seen you somewhere before." Then he swiveled the rifle over towards the hillside, where a group of deer lingered. He squeezed the trigger and the barrel issued a loud report.

One of the deer in the distance shivered in its tracks, then its legs collapsed and it slumped over. The others fled in all directions. Pleased with himself, the man looked at him and laughed.

"Dinner! Go get the carcass and throw it back in the truck," he barked to his companions. "You, follow me. And give me the keys to that wagon."

Cooper had no options. He was scared, and pissed at himself. For not seeing this coming. He dug into his pocket and handed the man the car keys. When he wasn't watched, he scanned the woods nonchalantly, but saw no sign of Mikaela, Amy, and Turk.

The man made him walk in front.

"What's your name?" he grunted.

"Shane Cooper."

"Alright, Cooper. You run for it, I'll shoot you in the back. No hesitation. Kapow! We're going to take everything you own, then you're going to work for us. *Unnerstand*? You know how it is here in the valley, labor is in short supply. Its tough to stay alive. Tough to make ends meet." Then he giggled. He seemed out of his gourd too, which made Cooper believe they could escape.

What a crazy world this is. Absolutely nuts. Then he thought,

Blow. Blow now...

He had Mount Rainier in mind. He wanted the primary eruption to happen *now*. Then he could run for it, fetch the others. And the bulk of this vermin would be wiped from the surface of the earth.

"Hey this doesn't make any sense," Shane said. "You should be getting your ass out of this region. Not wasting your time with me. The big blow from Rainier is coming, anytime..." It was then the butt of the rifle came down on the back of his head. Cooper felt the burst of pain and saw a shower of sparks before he blacked out and pitched forward into the long grass.

75

CHAPTER 17

"Is this the one?" he heard. An older woman's voice. His head pounded with a dull ache. His vision was blurry. The voice had a smoker's husky tone.

He leaned forward, lifting his head off a wall, focusing his eyes.

"I'm Gladys." She paused, expectantly, as if formal introductions were in order.

"Shane. I'm not from around here." He tried to bring the rest of the room into focus. He tried to find Beatrice, and the others.

"I'm trying to get home asap, so if you can..." He shuffled his feet, but they were restrained at the ankles. He heard a male howl of pain through sheetrock walls, but Gladys pretended not to notice it.

"This is *my* place Mr. Shane, my palace. Welcome." This grandiose reference was followed by a phlegmy laugh.

When he was sure he wasn't still unconscious, having a nightmare, he took a good look at her. Jeans, brand-new spotless white tennis sneakers; a flowered, buttoned-down shirt with a cheap red ribbon on the breast pocket. Pouffy hair and a wrinkled, late-middle-aged, not unfriendly face.

"I got you a cup of tea, a bottled water, and a hot-dog. How's that sound?" The phlegmy laugh came again. "It took me a minute, or so, until I figured out that you're the one who's been spearing my boys. With that crossbow of yours, over in the corner there. What are you, The Last of the Mohicans?"

He saw his weapon, in a cluttered pile of varied belongings. He wanted to sprint to it, seize it, and head for the exit, but for the zip-tied ankles.

"Apparently, you're pretty good at shooting. But these guys are like sons to me, and killing them well...I can't abide that. No, not at all.

"You must be smart, skilled. I'm trying to figure out how I can use that. You see, we're a *team* here. That's why we're still around, during the catastrophe. Hell and high water has broken loose, in case you haven't noticed. Polite society has failed–everyone else is gone. No police, fire, Army, ambulances, hospitals. Maybe a little like Katrina, remember that? The people were scared. Every man for himself. The unfortunate, the desperate. You don't want to find yourself in that category. The unprepared."

I always prepared, he thought, with more than an ounce of regret. "We're filling the void," she added, as if she had to explain her gang to him.

Cooper thought, *Power loves a vacuum. Or is it venality and crime?*

He looked around. He felt behind his head to the lump, which seemed to grow in his fingers. The place was some kind of warehouse. "Where is this?"

"Don't you recognize it? Why, it's America's emporium, everyone's favorite go-to weekend destination. Walmart. We've occupied the Walmarts, and the Lowe's, and the Best Buys. Whatever's left. The Whole Foods, *never liked that place,*" she said as an afterthought. "But alas, the food has run low. We're emptying the last of the shelves and food-supply trucks. When that's all gone, we'll just have to, well, scavenge what we can."

"You just got clobbered by that lahar."

"Not everything," she said.

"Where's Beatrice?"

"You mean the gentle old lady? Beatrice...she *seems* a Beatrice. We've got her in the pen...pardon me, a *room*...yonder over on the other side. It's where you'll be sleeping."

He reached over on the floor where a man had placed the food on a paper plate, and began chewing the hot dog slowly. He sipped the tea in a Styrofoam cup. Might as well.

"Have you looked at the sky lately?" he said, as Gladys still lingered.

"For what, divine inspiration?"

"Rainier's just getting started. Those lahars, they came from minor eruptions. The big one's coming; no one's going to survive that. It'll wipe out everything in this valley, like a nuclear bomb. Those dark plumes, they presage a massive eruption." He finished the hot dog, kept going with the inspiration. "You better move everything out of here. Get closer to the coast."

"How kind of you, to look after our welfare."

He shrugged and kept eating. "When are you going to take this thing off my feet, so I can move to your pen."

"Soon. We have plenty of work to do. You're going to be involved. I don't believe in wasting brains and brawn, but you have to know who the boss is. Who's the boss?"

He looked at her sullenly. She smiled, wrinkles spreading from the corner of her mouth, eyes narrowing. She turned to shuffle away, with two other men in tow. A subset of the men walking around, seemingly with jobs to do, like in any old Walmart, had their faces painted. It was unsettling; a mad costume party.

"By the way, Gladys," he said, still blurry to the point where his voice sounded, to him, like a mumble. "What's with the white makeup?"

"Our brand."

Soon enough, two guys sauntered up, grabbed him by the elbows, and dragged him into a nearby room, full of other captive people. He made a note of where his crossbow leaned against a wall, hoping they wouldn't move it. He felt naked without it, and everything else, like his trekking gear and Swiss knife.

He was too light-headed to resist, but that would come later, he vowed.

When the two guys dropped him on the floor, one of them drew out a hunting knife. Cooper wondered if the lunatic was going to cut him. But in a twisted way he believed Gladys, that she was saving his talents for later. The man laughed, bent down, then severed the zip-tie on his ankles; then they both left and locked the door behind them.

He lay a moment under the flickering fluorescents, then stiffly got back on his feet.

He thought he'd find Beatrice crying and distraught. But he saw her quietly leaning against a wall across the room, sunglasses on, appearing stoic and dignified.

"Beatrice!" he whispered hoarsely, walking over to her. A smile crept across her face. "It's Shane."

"I knew," she said. They hugged.

"We're getting out of here. Soon. I'm taking you with me. I don't know who the fuck this Gladys whacko thinks she is, but she's going to get us all..." Then he realized he was venting his own anxiety and only making matters worse for Beatrice. Yet, she read his mind.

"Don't worry," she said. "This man, he's been telling me everything about this place." She nodded her head to a man who sat glumly against the wall nearby. "He took me under his wing when he realized I was sight-impaired. I have faith in my fellow man. She is, of course, the Gladys I was telling you about; with the lengthy rap sheet, and list of grievances and resentments towards the local authorities.

"One thing you'd be interested to know."

"What?" Cooper began to feel his head clear.

"They weren't able to start my car. The Subaru."

"You mean back on the dirt road, with the horses?"

"Yeah. And I left a second set of keys under the front seat. Yes I did. You can be sure of that."

CHAPTER 18

According to Beatrice's friend, Gladys commanded a sizable labor force. They had commandeered Walmart's truck fleet, and were using captive labor to loot and load the trucks with the contents of every mall and warehouse in the valley. They planned to sell the stuff on the black market in California and Mexico. They were scooping up new people, kidnapped along the way.

There were rumors that a man had been beaten to death and hung from a pole in the parking lot, as an example to the rest.

Others said that Walmart refrigerators contained dozens of bodies. Some of them killed for storage. Cooper didn't believe that part; he chose not to. He figured they were wild-eyed rumors.

Cooper knew the lahar had probably killed thousands, but that didn't completely explain the emptied out towns they'd encountered.

He guessed the room they occupied was some kind of

staging area. There was no furniture. Or windows. So he slumped down and leaned with his back against a wall, beneath a jaundiced, flickering ceiling lamp. He wondered, and regretted, how he'd ended up in this sorry place. The string of events–if only he hadn't taken that climbing job. He could still be at home in Telluride, reading but only reading about these horrors on the news, maybe even in the arms of Alexis. He wouldn't have fallen into the clutches of an opportunistic psychopath. That only pissed him off. It felt like failure. But he realized, this was also a defeatist train of thought. It wasn't going to help him escape.

A man about Cooper's age stood nearby, pacing, on pins and needles, like everyone else.

"How long have you been stuck here?" Cooper asked.

"Since yesterday. I came over from Tacoma, looking for my girlfriend...and my dog."

"Did you find 'em?"

"No. I didn't have a chance to. These goons took me off the highway." The man had a neatly trimmed black beard and hair, faded jeans, sneakers. He was dressed "academically casual." He made Cooper think of Mikaela and her Egyptian boyfriend.

"Is your name Shakir?"

"No, Philip. Yours?"

"Shane. What was happening in Tacoma? That's where I'm headed, or trying to."

"I don't know, exactly."

"What do you mean, you don't know? You just told me you came from there."

"I mean, it was a normal reaction when I was leaving. People saw Rainier erupting. There was panic, gridlock. Voices on radio and cable saying to sit tight and 'await further instructions.' About half the city was trying to leave; the other half thought it was cool to ride it out, didn't think Tacoma or Seattle was affected, or they couldn't leave because they didn't have a car. Now, I couldn't tell you what's happening. The lahar could have gone that far. The situation is fluid."

82

No pun intended, Cooper thought.

"Did you see any trucks, helicopters, Army troops, anything like that, on your way over here?"

"None."

"Odd. The valley's been virtually empty since I got here. Very odd..."

"Maybe they got diverted," Philip quipped. "I've heard that all the valleys radiating from Rainier have been destroyed; 360 degrees."

"Christ. That's probably it."

"I thought the most I'd be doing is seeking higher ground from the lahars. I was trying to reach my girlfriend by cell phone; couldn't. Hopefully, they made it to Seattle. I heard the lahar warning signal go off in Sumner. An eerie sound, disturbing. You don't have a lot of time, maybe 30 minutes. A lot of people didn't make it."

"I'm afraid of the big one," Cooper said. "What if Rainier really blows, in a major eruption? We'll all be goners."

"Rainier isn't like Mount St. Helens," Philip said, shifting into an expert mode. "It doesn't have the massive lava dome buildup. So it's less likely to have the kind of eruption that's like a nuclear bomb, obliterating everything within 20 miles. The lahars are bad enough, though. What Rainer has is a lot of hydrothermically altered rock. This is sulfur that mixes with water and makes sulfuric acid, which degrades the rock into a kind of clay. That mixes with the massive amounts of snow and ice in Rainier's glaciers, and you have the perfect cocktail for a lahar, which even a minor eruption, like this one, sets off. Like the Osceola Mudflow, 5,600 years ago. That made it all the way to Puget Sound."

"Are you a scientist?"

"I write G.I.S. software. I had to research the Cascades once. It was interesting, *then*."

The explanation made Cooper's head spin, more than it was already. He exhaled heavily. "Do you know where we are now?"

"Just outside the city of Puyallup. We're still in the

lahar zone, right in the bull's eye. Do you have any food?"

"No."

Cooper stole a glance at Beatrice. Chatting with another woman, she seemed to be holding it together. He felt responsible; he didn't want her to be drawn into the hideous plans of these lunatics. She wasn't able to do all the physical work, because of her blindness. Any escape plans had to include Beatrice.

"When we get out of here," Cooper said. "You can come with us."

"How are you planning to do it?"

"I don't know yet."

At around dusk, a group of louts came into the room and moved them, like a herd of sheep, into a large, emptied out conference area, where they slept on the equivalent of wrestling mats. Cooper couldn't sleep; he rolled over and over fitfully, until he finally got up. Pissing had to take place in a trash bin tucked into the corner; it smelled putrid and tart. No one guarded the locked door; they appeared to have fallen asleep. He walked over and looked out a window and saw only impenetrable darkness, with a few fires licking in the distance.

He wondered what Mikaela, Amy, and Turk were doing. He was grateful they hadn't been seized, and he mulled over what Beatrice had said about the car.

He didn't want to spend another day in this prison. It made the devastated landscape outside beckon like freedom.

CHAPTER 19

The following morning, Cooper was brought onto the roof of the building with a group of captive men. A stocky thug with lurid tattoos on each side of his bald head grunted orders at them. It was scary, the unrestricted authority given to bulky nitwits.

Cooper contemplated hurling him off the rooftop, but resisted the temptation. He bottled up his escape plans until the right time.

They were supposed to rip out the copper pipe from the Heating, Ventilation, and A/C machines that nearly covered the rooftop. It was back-breaking work, on breakfast which consisted of peanuts and a rotten banana, but he was grateful, in a grudging way, to be outdoors and to get a higher view of their position.

On his way out of the conference room, and to a flight of steps that led to the roof, he spotted his crossbow. It was in the same place, leaning against the wall amongst the clutter.

From the rooftop, he looked at the sky. The sun fought

through a yellow, sulfurous haze, which edged west, toward the sea. He ran his fingers along a railing that encircled the rooftop, and came away with a peppery brown stain. He wondered what it would do to their lungs.

The view, he expected, would answer some of his questions, such as why this building and its environs were still standing. He spotted the lahar just over the railing, not 200 yards away. It was dark green, like moss, and reflected the muted sunlight with the swampy glint the slime on a rock would. It looked like the surface of another moon, but for the trashed human artifacts embedded in it.

It was pockmarked with pulverized debris, including the steeple of a smashed church, the roadbed and guardrails torn off a bridge; and a chunk of a movie marquee. It carried endless trees. Whole forests had been peeled from their roots and rode partly on the lahar's surface, like a giant run of logs on the Mississippi.

The lahar extended west as far as he could see. It was bigger than the others he'd seen, deeper and wider; 50-feet deep in places and a mile wide, at least. The bulk of it was no longer moving, yet closer to its source he could see blobs of the volcanic toffee slowly flowing and feeding the back end of the lahar, like the viscous final drippings from a paint bucket.

Pops and fiery outbursts marred its surface. Where these occurred, the lahar would stay on fire, like burning ocean oil from a sunken destroyer.

It took a path just south of them, and off to the other side, forming a fork. So where were they going to move to from here, he wondered, including Gladys and her trucks full of plunder?

The idiot with the tattooed head stood off to the side, lightly tapping a sawed-off shotgun on his thigh. "OK get working!" he shouted hoarsely.

One group of men loosened the joints on the pipes; another group, which Cooper was a part of, ripped them out and carried them downstairs to the parking lot.

When Cooper got down there with a load, which they

put on wheelbarrows, he saw Beatrice. They'd included her in a kind of assembly line, passing boxes of stuff to be loaded in the back of a truck. He shouted out to her, said he was okay, and to hang in there. As long as he knew her whereabouts, and they didn't scurry her off to an unknown fate, then they could escape together.

One time, they announced a break, and they were all allowed to gather around a barrel of brackish water for a drink. He found her, hugged her, and told her to get ready to move that night.

CHAPTER 20

Mikaela crouched in the underbrush, holding Turk down by the scruff near his ears. She told Amy to stay where she was, behind a tree. Luckily, Amy didn't protest, but viewed the proceedings intently. From the woods, Mikaela watched one of the men fail to start the car. The first truck drove off with Shane and Beatrice in the back. Then the man got out of the Subaru, kicked the front door closed angrily, got into the second pickup, and they drove away.

Mikaela softly swore to herself. When they saw the trucks disappear over a rise, they came out of hiding and walked back across a field to the car. She was hoping the stupid lug had left the keys in the ignition, but no such luck. But she located most of their provisions in the back. In his rush to leave, the idiot had left a lot of good stuff in the car, including Shane's rucksack. But not his crossbow. She put his rucksack on her own back, grabbed her gym bag, and got prepared to hike to that town they'd seen in the distance.

She felt like crying. She figured Cooper and Beatrice

would be killed by the crazies. That might have been the last they'd see of them, but she held out hope that if she got a ride back, maybe in the same direction of the trucks, she could find them.

She didn't want to upset Amy; she'd hold off on crying until she was alone.

She thought it was weird that the trucks drove back in the direction of the giant lahar path. Maybe that was a good thing. Maybe the two pickups would hit an impasse, and they'd have to turn around and come back in this direction. They'd see Cooper and Beatrice again.

Amy was clambering around the nooks and crannies of the car interior, gathering her dolls and other things. Turk stood with two front paws planted on the sill of the open car door.

Mikaela never would have thought that Amy could find something Mikaela couldn't herself. But Amy suddenly leapt up with a gleeful look and a set of keys in her hand. She'd found them under the passenger seat. Mikaela hugged her, then seized the keys and tried to start the car. It made the same chugging noise, but wouldn't catch. Close but no cigar.

Mikaela reached under the dashboard and popped the hood latch. Maybe, just maybe, she could find out what was wrong with the engine. She had a boyfriend in high school who was a grease monkey under cars. He showed her a lot of stuff, when she could focus long enough to listen. She walked to the front of the Subaru and propped up the hood. Her first thought was the battery, but it and the car overall was relatively new. It didn't seem rusted or degraded; the engine parts themselves were dusty from the wild ride they'd had down the dirt road. She remembered something else her boyfriend, his name was Davis, told her: *start-up problems usually aren't a problem with the distributor cap, but if all else fails, wipe off any excess moisture on the cap.*

She was afraid the starter was blown and they would be walking, but lo and behold, removing, wiping down, and reinstalling the distributor cap worked its magic. The car

89

started back up. Along with a tremendous sense of relief, she felt like a real Fix-It Girl.

"Turk!" she cried out. "Come on back here!" Turk had wandered back up the road in the direction the deer and horses had gone. Amy was half-way between the dog and the car, meandering aimlessly toward her loyal friend. Mikaela watched her for a moment, silently. The wind caught her long blond hair, a doll clutched in one hand. She wore the same dress of the last few days, now torn around the edges and soiled by their ordeal. It seemed a lonesome tableau, the country girl, set against the blackened horizon and blasted landscape. *What a strange trip it's been for her*, she thought. More of a nightmare than a childhood. *I'll do anything I can to get her back to safety*. But she couldn't stop thinking about Shane, and Beatrice.

She rounded up both dog and girl, they piled into the car, and Mikaela drove back up the road in the direction the trucks had gone.

CHAPTER 21

He couldn't take it anymore. The thug had been egging him on. It had only taken one afternoon. One side of himself said, *Take it for the time being—you'll be out of here soon.* The other half sought justice for this bullet-headed nitwit who kept poking him with the butt of his gun and kicking at him. Finally he reached up and grabbed the guy by the throat with his powerful grip, standing there on the rooftop under a weak, filtered sun.

When the guy tried to tuck the barrel of the shotgun into Shane's ribs, he head-butted him on the bridge of his nose. Dark red blood spurted straight out, and as the bellowing man fell backwards, an airborne bloody spray striped across her white sneakers. Gladys, Shane hadn't noticed, was standing at their side with one of her minders. When the blood stained her sneakers, the face of the guy standing next to her went white as a sheet.

"Take this guy here, and string him up," she muttered, her eyes narrowing. Her eyeballs themselves, however, seemed to mist over, as though the bloodied sneakers reminded her of something unbearably sad. She pulled a white handkerchief out of her pocket and handed it to her minder, who ran off to wet it. Then he returned, knelt down, and furiously scrubbed the blood stain on Gladys's sneakers.

A gust of cinders blew over the rooftop, warm and unnatural. It was as if the air and the landscape had reverted to a distant geological epoch. The bullethead with a broken nose stood up unsteadily, then he and another thug seized Cooper by each of his upper arms and dragged him roughly across the rooftop toward the stairs.

He felt like he could have broken free and ran, but he was afraid they'd take revenge on Beatrice, or shoot him in the back. Or both.

"Down in the courtyard!" he heard Gladys, her voice pinched and high-pitched.

Mikaela drove the car down the dirt road until they reached the rise, then she pulled over to the gravelly side. This was the place where they'd sped in the other direction, behind the stampeding animals. She had to plot a route down, and eventually, out of the valley. Turk followed her outside the car; he stepped gingerly down into a dry thicket to lift his leg on a rock. Then he sniffed the air, still as a statue.

Mikaela gazed over the battered valley; thousands of acres of productive farmland were now plowed-over and buried by the vast mudflow. The region seemed soaked in a toxic molasses.

The uneven wreckage was lit here and there by pillars of sunlight. There was no electricity, except for a few spots winking in the distance. But for their headlights, they'd be enveloped in pitch-black darkness soon.

She could see where the lahar had forked and moved in two directions, sparing structures and one road. The road led away from an island of buildings; she could see two or three trucks, heading west. That's where she needed to go, to the island.

The lahar had dammed the rivers to the east. A lake grew in the valley behind the berm- and concrete-like walls of lahar. She knew, at some point, it would flood; the valley to the west would be inundated.

Mount Rainier took up the eastern horizon, regal and domineering for so long, but now dwarfed by a pluming ash cloud.

The pickups with their captive friends could only have gone in one direction. The Subaru still had enough gas.

Turk crawled back into the car, and curled up beside Amy.

In a moment of reflection, listening to the silence, Mikaela thought of Shakir. They'd spent a long weekend together, not long ago, in the Idaho countryside. How different the world was then. How dismissive of its flaws she was; its pain. She could lose herself in escapism, relaxing with a lover. She could sit in a jacuzzi under Idaho's starlit evening, thinking of nothing but the cold vapor drifting off of the bubbling waters; Shakir's warm, giving smile in the steamy air.

Then, like an apple half eaten and left on a fence post in the sun, the world turned, like Rainier's floral river valleys, to rot.

Mikaela got into the idling car. She glanced at the gas gauge; she had half a tank. Possibly 200 miles, she calculated. A voice, one motivated by raw survival, urged her to turn around, head for that town they'd seen. But she pulled the car back onto the road and let it roll downhill toward the open highway.

She drove back into the ruins and the giant, half-baked lahar. Cooper was down there somewhere.

CHAPTER 22

They had him bound by each wrist with rope. Then a couple of guys on the other end of the rope winched him partway up a flagpole. He was hanging by his arms alone. It was in a courtyard, near the entrance to a warehouse. Maybe Walmart had made its employees recite the Pledge of Allegiance there.

Gladys tacitly supervised. With the dark beard and the long hair he'd grown over the last week and change, he felt like a crucified Jesus. As they winched him, to the sound of a creaky weather vane, his feet left the ground and he felt a profound pressure on his arms and shoulders.

One of the men on the other end of the rope chuckled; his partner turned to him and barked "Shut the fuck up!" with a hint of empathy. Gladys walked closer to inspect the work, with an air that she was busy, ready to move on to better things. She stood just beneath his dangling legs.

"What the *hell*," Cooper grunted, feeling gravity drive the air out of his lungs. "...happened to you?"

"...To become this?"

She was silent for a moment, weighing the question.

"None of your business."

An hour passed. Cooper's throat was raw, his tongue passed over the cracked lips. His legs felt like lead, tearing down at his shoulder tendons. He'd ceased glancing at the faces of the meek who wandered past on their various laborious missions. The sun went down. It was a red, toxic sunset, lit by sulfurous fumes. He didn't think he'd make it through the night.

"Water!" he croaked. "Water!"

"Just a minute," he heard, the voice incongruously nonchalant.

It was one of the guys who'd strung him up the fucking pole. He hovered in front of Cooper's head, standing on something, and lifted a ladle to his lips. Shane guzzled at the ladle and spilled half of it down his chin. His sweaty body hung limp and shirtless, the muscles glistening, the feet and legs flexing weakly.

The man quietly gave him another ladle full.

"How you holding up?" he whispered.

"Shitty."

"I might be able to take you down, soon."

"When?"

"Let the others fall asleep..."

"Don't take your time at it."

"Wait." It had gotten a lot darker. The man reappeared, this time with a tree stump. They were using it to cut wood on. He propped up Cooper's feet with it. Immense relief flooded over him.

"Thanks," he grunted.

"I don't want to see you die. Don't misunderstand my intentions here. I'm a prisoner, just like you."

"So cut me down and we both go, with my friend Beatrice."

"Who's that?"

"The blind one."

"Oh, shit."

"What?"

"It's not that easy."

"Why?"

"I'd have to get the other chick...what did you say, Beatrice? Out of that building over there. It'd be hard enough for just me and you. And if they caught me, she'd throw me to her dogs."

"You mean she has packs of dogs?" The man handed him another ladle of water.

"No. They're human. Feral. They're actually worse than her few guard dogs."

"What *is* wrong with her? Was she just *born* bad?"

"Well the story goes..." He was in a low whisper now.

"Gladys was running a numbers parlor out of her first laundromat. Young. Ambitious. She had twin girls. She used to bring them to work. One day, she left a cigarette butt in an ash tray near some linen, and went down the block to collect a vig from the guys who ran numbers for her. The linen caught fire, and, you know what old laundromats are like, they're almost as bad fire-wise as dry-cleaning joints. The place was ablaze. They couldn't get to the kids. She came back to the burning building holding two brand-new pairs of white sneakers for them. Now she's all about taking in the damaged off the streets. And sneakers. That was about 30 years ago."

The sun went down; the lights around the building clicked off one by one. Cooper's new "friend" was going to be replaced when his shift was over. Unfortunately, by the lug whose nose he'd broken. In the darkness, a distant set of headlights illuminated the gloomy courtyard.

96

CHAPTER 23

The night settled down around the car, and Mikaela had a good cry. It wasn't that it had all become too much for her; she wouldn't take it that far. She needed a good cry like she needed a good sleep.

Amy and Turk lay in the half darkness on the back seat. She drove along slowly, toward the valley and the lahar, wet eyes blurring the murky evening. She hit the dust on the windshield with the washer and the wipers. She knew this road would end somewhere, massively blocked by the remains of the lahar. But she'd seen that one working road from above; and the few trucks, heading west toward Tacoma.

She rubbed the tears off her cheeks with the bottom of her hand, the other gripping the steering wheel. A stark, windswept dirt road with rocks and the gleam of a startled deer. Bad things that happen, like when your sister drowns, never really leave you, she thought. They hang around like a mood drug up by the colors of a certain sunset, or the smell of cooking. Then the curtain drops over you for a while.

97

It's like dealing with the complete destruction of a human settlement, and a sadistic gang. A cry staunches the wound, then it'll be time to find Cooper and Beatrice. If she can.

She stopped the car in the breakdown lane, wiped her wet nose with her shirtsleeve, killed the headlights. She got into the back seat with Amy, who'd fallen asleep. Mikaela hugged her with one arm, and stroked Turk with the other. Amy moved her head and opened her eyes. Her face was all sleepy and mopey. "I love you," Mikaela said quietly, sinking her head into Amy's soft mass of unruly hair.

"I know," Amy said, looking askance, still in dreamland. It crossed Mikaela's mind that Amy needed a bath and a shampoo *badly*; but they all did. She almost got one at Beatrice's house.

She still had the pistol stuffed into the shiny warm-up coat she'd worn the whole time. Two slugs left, she thought; you can hug an innocent girl and think of putting slugs into men at the same time. It was becoming easy. Too so.

She weighed the information she was going to give Amy, then, "I'm going to look for some food, and you and Turk are going to be alone for a few minutes."

"When?"

"We're going to drive for a little bit first. Can you keep Millie and Tom company while I'm gone? I don't want to hear them complaining."

Amy mustered a smile. "*They* don't complain. They're not like real people! They're just *dolls*!"

"Oh *really*? Now when did that happen? I always thought Millie and Tom were real. They're well enough real to me."

"They've always been, just dolls...but I still like them." Amy reached over where Millie and Tom lay semi-crushed and wedged into the end of the backseat. "I still *like* them. They're still my friends! Oh you don't understand."

"Yes I do. Now, can you, Turk, Millie, and Tom be brave for me, when I go look for food? You'll have to stay in the back seat and not let Turk out. I'm afraid he'll run away. I'll only be a few minutes." Then Mikaela thought of other possible scenarios, but didn't think this poor little girl could digest them.

"Do you promise?" Amy said pleadingly.

"Scout's honor."

"*Who's* honor?"

"Just an expression. I promise. I promise. I promise."

Mikaela got back into the front seat. She'd left the engine idling. The headlights went on, and she rolled back onto the gravel. Within a mile she came to the northern boundary of the lahar.

CHAPTER 24

She drove down out of the foothills, and when she reached the bludgeoned valley, she could no longer see over the lahar to the surviving road. But she knew the lone highway was out there somewhere.

Her headlights illuminated a small mountain of debris that the lahar had carried across the landscape. It blocked the rest of the dirt road. She stopped, got out of the car, folded her hands across her chest. From above, she'd seen the lahar path fork, with one of the tines of the fork shorter than the other. That was west of where she stood, and not far.

In the sepulchral evening, the windy silence, she felt like they were the last humans left in the valley. She'd make her way slowly along the short tine of that fork, then try to hook around onto the highway again. She thought the car was up to it.

The headlights stabbed into the gnarled debris; she walked in front of them back to the idling car.

The guy with the tattooed head kicked the feet supports out from under him, and Cooper was left hanging again by the rope. He grunted as his body jerked down on his arms and shoulder sockets, the rope biting into his wrists. The peon had a set of bandages across his nose; his voice came out muffled.

"I ought to kill you right now for what you did to my nose. Fuckin' sucker punch head-butt." He sipped something from a Styrofoam cup and talked into the night. "Gladys wouldn't let me though. So I guess you're a lucky fuck. You won't be too good in the morning anyways, if you're still alive. I'm just going to leave you twisting in the wind, *buddy*."

At the end of an alley, connected to the courtyard, Cooper had sensed what he thought were headlights flash across the dark sky, then click off. Now in the darkness, he saw the awkward amorphous form of the idiot wander behind him, so he couldn't see him anymore. They were alone out there.

Then he heard a struggle, like two people grappling but trying not to make any noise.

There was a move that she would never use in a bonafide MMA match because it cuts the blood off instantly to the brain. It's called a blood choke. She had no such qualms here.

When she got to the end of the alleyway, a lone bulb weakly lit the courtyard. She saw a man hanging from a pole by his arms. It was dark, but he had Cooper's hair. She halted for a minute, sizing up the situation. A building full of people, captives and bad ones, but only one guard. She saw a stocky guy sitting on the ground. He stood up and ambled sleepily closer to Cooper. His back to her.

She felt for the gun, and the Swiss knife. She might need both, she thought. But she wanted silence.

When she hit him from behind she had both forearms

101

locked around his carotid artery, powered by muscular shoulders. She wrapped her legs from behind around the chubby guy's waste. The blood choke, it was like pushing a button. With nothing going to the brain, he flopped over like a sack of potatoes, lights out.

Maybe it wasn't such a bad idea back in the gym, when her mentor Vincent taught her a few "no holds barred" quasi-legal moves. She took out the knife, Cooper's, and unsheathed it.

"Shane, baby, it's me. You okay?" She moved the wooden stump over to where he was hanging, and clambered on top of it. She went to work on a frenzied cutting of the rope. It only took a minute for the sharp knife to sever the cord. He dropped down onto the rough ground and composed himself for about 20 seconds. He felt like crap; everywhere a pulsating bruise.

"I'm okay. I can't believe it's you!" he said in a hoarse whisper. He felt around his sore shoulders. At least his arms were still in their sockets. "Where are the others?"

"In the car."

His shirt had been hurled to the side; he found it and pulled it roughly over his sweaty torso. The building was still quiet, until they noticed Cooper's guard complaining bitterly as he staggered to his feet. He stood, a hulking presence in the low light, like Frankenstein.

"I'm gonna tear your fuckin' head off," he mumbled when he saw Mikaela, but couldn't finish the sentence before she spun and side-kicked him smack in the testicles. Groaning, he bent forward like a pretzel, holding onto his abs. He was on the ground for good, face first, out cold, when she followed through with a solid right to the face, further rearranging it around the existing bandage.

"I almost feel sorry for him," Cooper whispered. "Wait here!"

He sprinted to the building's exit, where the previous guard told him he'd prop the door open. He'd promised, if Cooper would take him out of there. Cooper found the door

102

open a crack, ran in and down the hallway, stealthily through one of the doors, until he located the crossbow. It was still in a pile of random belongings where he'd seen it before. *Hallelujah*, he thought. The quiver was still two-thirds armed. They weren't too smart around there. The only business left was Beatrice.

He ran down the hall, away from the exit door, looked around the corner; nothing. Then he heard a commotion. He noticed Mikaela at the exit door to the building, waving at him frantically.

There was the guy who'd given him water, the first guard, coming through another distant door, too loudly, gripping Beatrice by the arm.

CHAPTER 25

A man, ghoulishly powdered white in the half
darkness, came bursting through the door behind them. He
grabbed the guard first by the collar, spun him around, and
they tussled. Beatrice broke free and took long, confusing
strides, until Cooper grabbed her hand.

"Beatrice it's Coop! Run!" Holding hands, they
sprinted down the hallway toward Mikaela. She held the door
open for them.

Cooper saw the handgun in Mikaela's hand, extended
down by her thigh. He took one look behind him and saw the
white-faced pursuer break free. The man had a handgun
stuffed into the back of his trousers; he reached behind and
yanked it free. Thoughts raced through Cooper's mind: he
didn't want them to be shot, but neither did he want this
sleeping complex to wake up and come down on them.

He saw Mikaela push the door open wider and gesture
wildly with the hand holding the handgun to go faster. "Go,
go, go!" she cried. "We have to get out of here! We have to get

back to the car, and Amy!" Then a shot rang out and echoed in the hallway.

Turk's panting breath clouded up the window. He stood on the back seat tensed on four legs. He hadn't moved since Mikaela had run off in that direction. Once in a while, he'd give a short, puffy bark, and paw at the seat like a penned animal coiled to flee.

"Where *are* you?" Amy said to herself, sitting on her hands in the back seat. "It's taking too long! She said she was just going to get food! So where is she? What if Mikaela doesn't come back Turk? What if it's just me and you?" Mikaela hadn't told her what to do. Amy was too scared to sleep. It was pitch black outside, since Mikaela had shut off the headlights.

Amy reached over, took the flashlight, and fiddled with it. It clicked on, and the powerful beam reflected back at her from the window, like something else she wanted to run away from. That was enough; she unlatched the passenger door. Amy darted outside into the night, right behind Turk's leaping body. The flashlight beam stabbed around into the night until it hit the tree-tops, and the gutter of a building.

She heard a pop in the distance; men's busy, alert voices. She faced the walls of the windowless buildings with an alleyway between them. Behind her was the car, dark woods, and a road leading away. She couldn't believe Turk was running away from her. "Turk!" she cried out, breaking the gloomy silence around her. She aimed the flashlight at his form. "Come back here! Don't leave me!" She was scared, starved, tired, sad, all at once.

Turk's black torso disappeared into the lightless alley. She couldn't believe that he would leave her all alone! All she could do is follow him, calling out, quietly whimpering. She ran in her little sneakers and dress along the gravelly ground gripping Millie in her right hand, which she didn't even know she was doing. "Turk!"

It took everything she had to go into the alley.

Everyone was always leaving her! Getting dead. Or running away, too fast for her to catch.

Almost right away when she got to the end of the alley, she heard barking, snarling dogs. Some of the sounds she recognized as Turk's. Two shadows ran toward her. Growling and fighting and snapping commenced; she turned and ran as fast as she could in the opposite direction.

CHAPTER 26

Some guy in an adjoining room heard the gunshot in the hallway. He had two German Shepherds with him. When he got outside, with a T-shirt and unbuckled jeans, he saw the empty rope, two people running in the courtyard, and a dog. "G'on now! Go boys," he yelled at the two dogs, snapping on an outdoor lamp. They took off.

Cooper and Mikaela, both frazzled with adrenaline, part led, part dragged Beatrice toward the alley. She screamed at them, "Leave me!" but they ignored her. Then Cooper heard the dogfight behind him.

Turk had met one of the dogs in mid-air; they collapsed into the dirt in a whirl of flying fur, bared teeth, spit, and claws. The third dog joined in. "Keep going!" Cooper yelled back to Mikaela, who had Beatrice's sweaty hand. "Give me the gun!"

He strode up to the fighting dogs, aimed, and almost surgically, shot once, twice, and that was it for the ammo. Turk rolled off from the second dying dog, then got up, hind legs

107

first. Shaky, and bleeding. "You okay boy? C'mon!" Cooper still gripped the crossbow in his left hand. The guy who'd set the dogs on them buckled up his pants and stomped across the courtyard in the pale light.

Cooper expected *him* to pull a weapon, but he stopped at the two Shepherd bodies. He knelt down. Cooper and Turk trotted into the darkness of the alley; neither had much fight left in them.

Mikaela led them to the car. She still had the keys on her. "Goddammit where's Amy?" she hissed into the night. "Amy! Where are you! Amy's not here!" Cooper expected Gladys's troops to be on top of them at any moment.

"Turk, where's Amy?" Cooper asked, half expecting a rational answer. The dog's black coat gleamed with blood, sweat, slobber, and tensed muscle. He stood panting with the false grin of a battle-scarred mutt, slobber dripping off his jowls. Cooper tossed the gun onto the back seat. He felt crappy about the two Shepherds, but it couldn't have been helped. There was no way he had ever shot a dog before, or would have under any other circumstance. He urged Turk into the back seat; this time the dog, like a spent fighter, climbed arthritically and fell willingly onto the backseat cushions. He curled up and sighed.

Cooper backed out of the car and cupped his hands around his mouth. "Amy! Where the hell could she have gone? Hey Amy!" Mikaela had all but stuffed Beatrice into the front passenger seat, then got into the driver's side herself.

"Poor girl!" Beatrice said. "To be so young and a part of this! She must have wandered off a ways!"

Mikaela started up the car. "There's no way we're leaving without her!"

"Well, we gotta book out of here anyway, or we're all lost. Those morons will be down on top of us in no time. Let's head up the road, we'll look for her! Amy!" Cooper called out again. He leapt into the car and slammed the door. The Subaru started moving.

The black night was like a wall. You couldn't see past

much of a car length. No lights were on anywhere, and it was all dark woods. Going about half the speed Cooper thought they needed to, in order to put miles between themselves and Gladys, they stared out into the blackness looking for any sign of Amy–the beam of a flashlight, or headlights reflecting off a dress.

He knew they couldn't go too far; they'd reach a kind of point of no return. If that happened, he'd have to declare her, in an unspoken way, lost. Essentially abandoned–but that would never happen, he told himself. They were all in this together; it had been that way since the beginning. *Till death do us part.*

They went along the road and they'd all rolled their windows down and were calling out her name.

"Could she have been snatched by one of the goons back there?" Cooper speculated, over the back seat. Sleepless, and half-beaten, he felt like he was operating solely on high-test fumes. "While we were all preoccupied or tied-up? Maybe they took her; they have her back where we just came from." *God forbid*, he thought.

"No," Mikaela said. She seemed sure of herself. She gave off a vengeful, determined optimism. "Turk wouldn't have allowed it, or he would have followed them after they took her. They would have then shot him, and taken her. But Turk's still here. She's just wandered off, that's all. Dammit, she has this way of wandering off all the time!" Mikaela seemed choked up.

"The poor girl is just scared!" Beatrice agreed. "I don't blame her one bit!"

Turk had been licking his wounds, curled up in the back. Then he jumped up onto his hind legs all of a sudden, propped himself on the door with his front paws, and barked out the half-open window. Mikaela hit the brakes. Only trees swaying in the weirdly warm darkness, and a rushing sound; water.

The noise was like a river over rocks.

CHAPTER 27

Mikaela killed the headlights. She was out of the car in an instant. Turk barked two more times, in recognition, at the woods.

Cooper opened his door, stiffly exited, and stood by the side of the road with his crossbow. He was aware that they had pistols, with no ammo. They'd hardly gone a mile, maybe a mile and a quarter. He expected his captors to come barreling down the road at any second.

"Go find her Turk," he said. "Go find Amy. You smelled something. Go ahead boy!" The dog panted heavily, then barked in a way that was more like a release of air from the back of his throat. It was like an answer to the man's request. His brow furrowed; he stared into the dark trees, which hid the rushing water.

"Go on," Cooper said. "We're right behind you."

"Stay with the car!" Mikaela barked at him, over her shoulder.

"Why?"

"We need it! I can do this myself! Stay with the car!"
She was getting increasingly hard to say no to, Cooper thought.
With her fierce will, which only stiffened with the direness of
the consequences. Turk ran into the woods, like it was part of a
game.

"Alright alright go!" he said, waving an arm.

Mikaela strode into the woods. They could only see
Turk's tail; they won't lose him though, Cooper thought. He
comes when you call. He looked at Beatrice skeptically, then
back at the fleeing Mikaela.

"Don't be long!" he called out after her. "Be careful!"

A crashing of underbrush, then dog and woman
slipped into the darkness. Only the breezy noise of white water
came from the woods. Finally, a light clicked on way back in it.
A flashlight. The dot of light danced around, then it
disappeared, too.

"We should go with them; I don't trust this. It feels like
everyone's split up now, again. I don't like it–not one bit."

He began to pace, full of misgivings and exhausted
indecision. "I can't just wait in the car. That's not going to
work. These crazies are coming, we're going to have to step on
it, then that'll leave three not one of the others in the woods for
good." He felt a crazed energy, that high-test he ran on. His
legs wanted to fidget and run. He went back into the car to
fetch his backpack and things.

It reminded him of a journalist's photo after an aerial
bombing; dolls in the rubble. Tom lay on the back seat; he
snatched the doll and stuffed it into his backpack.

Beatrice got out of the car. A warm wind blew over the
road, carrying either dust, ash, or both. The road was still dark,
but he expected to see headlights coming at them, at any
moment. "A large river, rapids...it's close," Beatrice said. "I
hope Amy is alright. Where is the poor girl?"

"It could be the Puyallup River, or some smaller creek I
don't know anything about. Let's go!"

"I'll stay..."

"No. You have to come too." It'd be a death sentence

for her, if he left. He had a sneaking suspicion they may not make it back to the car.

It looked like run-off, a creek spontaneously formed. Turk stood next to it and barked, as if talking to it. A cool spray rose up smelling of sulfur and hard minerals. It cascaded down out of a jumble of rocks that climbed on the other side. Yet, not 15 feet away, Mikaela spotted a narrow torrent of the run-off emerging from an opening, as if it had already sculpted a hole through the rocks. This opening was topped by a natural bridge. She leapt up on it and scrambled across, hand over hand. She called Turk over the bridge. After a bit of hesitation, he came dutifully.

Once on the other side of the water, Turk picked up a scent and took off. She climbed up in pursuit of him. They were clambering over debris, recently deposited. It was scrambling in the grainy light, one hand gripping a flashlight, the beam reflecting back an ugly sheen. The rocks were wet with moist sand, a kind of slime. They made for awkward footing, and she was breathless, combined with all the other exertions, when they reached the top.

Turk's black form was more distinct now. He went over the crest. She clicked off the flashlight. "Amy!" she cried, dryly. "Amy, are you there? Amy? Where are you!" She began to cry silently, in a way that snuck up behind her. It was dredging up memories of Missy, a hollow, ageless, desperate longing, mixed with extreme fatigue. No amount of MMA training could prepare for this; beating up a 200-pound man, racing through the woods, going to the mat, emotionally.

Tears streaked down her cheeks. She wiped them off and put her hands on her hips.

"*Jesus Christ*," she declared out loud. She winced and said, "Where could that girl have gone?" She had a horrifying thought that they'd missed her driving that mile back there; they'd gone completely past her somewhere in the woods. She thought if she lost Amy, she'd sit down in the rocks with her head in her hands and never move again. Just die.

Then the sun came up. A fiery crack appeared in the

sky near the decapitated Mount Rainier. An orange halo around the fuming peak. Beautiful and holy in its own right. Vectors of sunlight crept across the rough terrain. They spread quickly, like a flowing tide.

Turk stood stock still, the black fur, crusted with dried blood, riffled in the breeze. He had a noble profile; she depended on him, like never before. He panted, then when he savored the scents in the wind, he stopped panting; his mouth firmed. He didn't blink.

She didn't know where to go. "What about it Turk?"

He looked over his shoulder in the other direction. Then she heard, "Mikaela!" It was Cooper, with his backpack and stuff, a short distance away. Coming up behind over the same route.

"I thought I told you...*what about the car?*" The words came out mumbled, he couldn't have heard them. It seemed, as of now, a non-issue. They were together. Then as the light bloomed and shifted around them, the terrain's features were revealed.

She saw a lone house in the distance.

CHAPTER 28

The house was tiny, yet the only intact manmade structure in view. Little house on the prairie, but in this case, it was little house in the wasteland.

"What the hell is this place?" Cooper said, to himself. "A moonscape...nothing more than that."

Turk looked back at Cooper. The dog seemed to relax and wag his tail slowly. Then he turned to look at the house again. He walked toward it, delicately choosing where he placed his paws over sharp, uneven ground. Mikaela followed, knowing that Cooper and Beatrice were right behind. The ground reminded her of a rugged coastline, in Maine or Hawaii.

Then it occurred to her that they may be walking on the huge lahar itself. It covered most of the valley, so it followed...but was it even possible? Wouldn't it still be hot?

The walk to the house was about a mile.

"Are you thinking what I'm thinking?" she said. They were bathed in low-angled sunlight; the ground beneath gleamed and crunched underfoot. It did seem an impossible, gross mishmash. Like the bottom of an industrial river that cities have dumped refuse in, then the river dries up and reveals its ugly contents. Everything was torn up and pressed together like a puzzle; pulverized stones and trees and chunks of tar and odd wedges of metal, ripped from buildings. Lots of machined wood; the debris from destroyed homes and buildings and roofs. She thought she walked over a storage tank. All of it glued together with mud.

"Um, is this the lahar?"

"Yeah, I think you got that right," Cooper said. He led Beatrice carefully.

"You've got to be kidding," Beatrice said, good-naturedly, as if aware of the burden of being held by hands on this rough surface. "We're walking, on that thing? From the mountain?" They were all fascinated, in a way, with being free of bondage, alive, and thrust feet first, as it were, into an oddity of Mother Nature.

"As bizarre as it sounds," Cooper added.

"I thought these things were steaming, molten?"

"Apparently they cool pretty fast. The lahars usually don't have red-hot lava. That comes at another time. They're mud and melt-water and rocks and all the junk they pick up. We're walking, basically, on a big garbage pile, from hell. Watch where you put your hands and feet."

Cooper caught up to Turk, reached down, scratched him behind the ear, which induced the dog to sit down gratefully. Then Cooper took the lead in their march toward the house. He looked quickly behind him toward the woods; nothing, but the river. They were alone.

He remembered what he'd seen in the house when he'd first dropped into the wreckage of the Puyallup Valley. Days ago, but it seemed like a month. He was alone, he'd lost his friends in the van, the first lahar had roared through. He was still scared shitless, uncertain of his chances, and thinking Rainier would go nuclear at any moment, or another lahar would take out the rest of the valley.

115

All he'd wanted was some food, provisions, maybe a rest. A breather, given what he'd gone through. This little house in the distance brought it all back to him. To the point where he didn't want to go there.

In fact, he was beginning to feel sick, the hot rim of a headache, an irritable indigestion. He figured it was lack of sleep; he tried to shrug it off.

That's when he heard a sound in the distance. Something in the wind, like that flagpole clanging back in Orting. But this was a regular high-pitched screechy sound, like "reek...reek...reek...."

They kept on walking, until they reached a point where the edge of the lahar stopped and tumbled down to what used to be the grassy lawn of a home.

The house had white flaking clapboards, a few falling down shutters, and a black shingled roof. It was a modest Cape in design, with an unpaved driveway going off to nowhere; a brick chimney stained with soot stuck up in the air. The vast majority of this rural neighborhood had been destroyed.

Turk stood stoically on the corniced edge of the lahar, nose in the air, as if searching for scents that weren't foul or redolent of death. Then he made his way carefully down.

In the breezy silence, Cooper could still hear, "reek...reek...reek." But not a bird could be seen.

CHAPTER 29

They reached the ground, after about 30 feet of a careful climb down over jumbled debris. The lawn was scorched grass and bare dirt. They faced the back of the house; a plastic child's tricycle, a fallen-down fence, a tipped-over grill. They all gathered at the bottom of the lahar, Cooper extending his hand for Mikaela and Beatrice. Turk began to walk to the front of the house, his thirsty tongue lolling out.

Cooper really wasn't feeling good. Something foreign and viral coursed through his system. He began to feel irritated; he tended to get mad at himself when he fell ill. It was another thing that felt like failure, as in allowing himself to be seized by Gladys.

"Reek...reek" he heard in the wind, picturing an old twisted weather vane.

Then Mikaela called out.

"It's Millie!" She ran to a spot on the lawn and seized the doll off it. She embraced it, clutching the doll to her chest like Amy would have. "My God!" Then she ran full tilt, and

117

they all followed to the front of the house.

When Cooper turned the corner, he saw the old swing-set, with two swings attached by metallic chains, and the little girl sitting on one of the swings. She kicked her legs up around the tattered dress, her blond hair blowing in the wind.

"Oh Amy!" Mikaela said, suddenly angry, and taking long strides.

Amy acted as if they weren't there at first. Then she began talking in between kicking her legs out, with the slim dirty sneakers she wore aimed toward blotches of blue sky.

"You...didn't...come...back...like...you...said...."

"So...I...went..."

Mikaela had reached her now. She couldn't stay mad. She was crying. She caught Amy on the back swing, stopped her swinging, and held on.

"Why did you leave me like that? Why? I told you to stay. Oh Amy, we thought we lost you!" Tears soaked her cheeks, which she tried to wipe away with the sleeves around her wrists. She hugged her tight and Cooper couldn't hear what she was saying anymore, murmurs into Amy's hair, with the little girl submitting passively to the embraces.

A salty wetness rose in his own eyes; he always got emotional when he got sick.

Then Amy said, out of the blue, "There's food in the kitchen. Inside...you should see it. I had some..." Cooper noticed that Beatrice had sat down on the grass. She hugged her knees and smiled beatifically. Her experiences, of existing on the edge of survival, and not seeing, seemed to have distilled in her an internal grace.

Turk wandered over to Amy and Mikaela, lazily wagging his tail, then when either of them leaned into his range, he'd give them a lick.

"It was you Turk. You found Amy. And Amy, I can't believe you just wandered off like that. Do me a favor, a big one," Cooper said. "Don't do that again. Ever."

Then, as he walked over to pet Turk, the sandy ground around the swing-set began to whirl. Moments later, he was groveling in the dirt, soaked in sweat, and he could hear Amy in the background, hollowly, say "You look white as a ghost!"

They led him into the house, through a broken, unlocked door, a cluttered kitchen, then onto a small, stiff couch. He collapsed on it and thrust his face into a throw pillow. How it all had come over him was shocking; he was weak as a kitten, sweating buckets. Then as soon as he closed his eyes he passed out.

He heard the voices of Mikaela and Beatrice; Amy's, temporarily complaining and crying, then nothing.

He was going down to that house again in the Puyallup Valley. He could feel his feet strike the ground on the hillside, gravity urging him downward; the palpable heft of his rucksack. He could see the bereft cluster of wooden homes spared from the first lahar, now in his dream, obscured by wisps of fog. He made his way down the hill, toward one of them.

He could hear, again, the woman's lusty cries from the second floor. The tone and volume was like working through labor pains. Against his will, the dream led him through that empty yard again, into the back screen door toward the woman's cries; up the dark stairwell, and then woozily along a hallway.

He paused at an open door. A bed, a woman lay in soaked, bloody sheets. She'd just given birth, she held a slimy mewling baby, very much alive, but still connected with the umbilical cord. The cord lay heavy, messily, and inapt on the sheets next to her.

"Get my husband!" she screamed.

"Where is he?"

"Downstairs...Get him! Now! Please!" He heard a deep, terrible voice from the floor below. He spun, then he woke up. He had a blanket over him, on the couch, and it was like emerging from an airless, pitch-black basement into sunlight.

CHAPTER 30

His tongue felt like a piece of velcro. It stuck to and pealed away from other parts of his mouth. He'd slept off at least some of this virus or bacteria that had swarmed his insides. He put one foot on the floor and steadied himself, a hand clinging to the couch's armrest. He draped the blanket over his shoulders like a shawl, and shuffled into the kitchen.

Mikaela was standing by the window. Sunshine filled the panes.

"Is there any water?"

"No, just some lukewarm O.J. We saved you some," she said to the window. She looked back at him. "How do you feel?"

"Like something Turk dragged in. I did sleep though."

"That's good."

He reached for the O.J. on the table and drained it. Flowing over his tongue, it tasted like the finest Champagne. The table was covered with the pickings of the kitchen. A bag of powdered milk, dry oatmeal, half-full cereal boxes; a

Morton's salt container, moldy orange cheese hanging out of shrink wrap, caky peanut butter, open and with a butter knife lodged in the middle of it. There was an old can of Nescafe instant coffee, a cellophane cylinder of Saltines, and a few plastic packages of beef jerky.

He was famished. "Do you mind?" he said. He scooped some Wheaties out of one of the boxes and nibbled them slowly.

"Any milk?"

"No."

"Didn't think so."

Beatrice sat at the table nearby. "Give me your hand."

He held it out for her; his arm felt tremulous. Her grip was gentle, firm, and dry. "Your forehead...?"

He bent down a bit, she placed her hand on his forehead.

"Yup, you're feverish; 102.5, 103.5, somewhere in there. I was afraid you had a 104 and up. You should sit in the sun, out there on the porch. We all should."

"You found good food," he said, still unsteady. "Bravoh."

He sat down in an empty chair. He seized a handful of stale Saltines and sequentially ate them. They were so stale they dissolved without chewing in his mouth. Turk, who'd been sitting in the corner of the room, ambled over to him and sat down. Cooper ran his hand down the back, felt the bones and the crusty blood along the fur.

"How are yah boy?"

"He's OK," Mikaela said. "Believe it or not, I found an old dog-food can and opened it for him. I almost saved it for us."

"Hah." That reminded him of Max eating the dog food, from *Mad Max*. "How long was I out?"

"A few hours," Beatrice said.

Cooper reached over, grabbed one of the jerkies. He struggled pathetically with the plastic. He remembered his rucksack and crossbow; in a feverish panic, he stood up.

121

Mikaela read his mind.

"They're leaning against the couch. Everything's there."

He went into the next room, rifled through the rucksack, and found his knife. *Mikaela thinks of everything,* he thought. *She looks after me.* He came back into the room and used the knife on the jerky, started chewing the leather-like piece. He sliced it in half and handed one half to Turk, who snapped at it then chewed vigorously.

Cooper poured a little salt from the Morton's on the jerky. He was starved, but the dry food was making him thirsty. He remembered he still had some aspirin in the med kit.

"We need to go back to the river," Mikaela said. "Fill some bottles."

"I can do that with you...where's Amy?"

"She's playing...upstairs," Mikaela said, rummaging under the sink.

"She found some little plastic people, and animals," Beatrice said.

"We're not letting her go outside, unless we're there," Mikaela added.

"Good idea." Cooper stood up and went to look out the window.

"I wonder where they went," he said. "The people who used to live here." He hadn't found any bodies in the house, but neither had he given it the complete once-over. The sun on his face, through the window pane, felt restorative, in a simple, natural way. The sky was egg shell blue, hazy, but less choked with ash.

He looked out upon a kind of stricken Great Plains; nothing stood, except for the choppy outlines of a few ruins. Nothing grew. Parts of the vast lahar gleamed wetly in the sun. The woods they had emerged from, he deliriously almost didn't remember that, were off the other side of the house.

He passed his hand over his forehead; it didn't feel quite so hot.

With the mild recovery came back his fear and concern.

Gladys and her cadre of louts were within about two miles. They must have discovered the car by now. That was gone; they had no transportation. The house was a refuge; but it was too wide open and vulnerable. Soon it would be night.

"I'll go get some water. I feel better. You should stay, Mikaela." She interrupted him.

"No, we all go together. From now on, everything's together."

He didn't have the will to resist her; he wasn't so sure he ever had it, even without this virus. He pet Turk by the window, feeling his heartbeat slow. That, and the cereal, the O.J., the Saltines–a marginal recovery. Comparatively, he was still weak as a kitten. After getting another Saltine and gobbing a chunk of the paste-like peanut butter on it, he went to the door to step into the sun.

"We have to gather everything we find here, that's usable, and bring it with us," Mikaela said, inspecting a collection of stuff she'd found under the sink. Cooper thought she was so exhausted she'd become robotic.

"Have you rested yet?"

"A bit..."

There were sponges, crusty powdered soap, a near-full bottle of propylene glycol. *So she realizes we have to leave soon, too,* he thought to himself.

"I'll look outside, see what I can find. Listen, you should crash, Mikaela. We have the time."

"Rest comes later."

Cooper returned to his pack, pulled out the med kit and an aspirin bottle, and chewed two on his way out. He still had the blanket around his shoulders. He carried the crossbow. He made a note to search the basement for anything they could use, including pistol ammo. That find, only if they were immensely lucky.

He was met with pleasant sunshine when he went out onto the wooden porch.

The swings on the swing-set moved lazily in a breeze. He heard Beatrice behind him, "I'm going to get Amy...she should come outside."

When he looked east, towards Rainier's gloomy, broken profile, he noticed a blue shimmer along the horizon. It resembled the contours of a coastline, where you can see the line of water reflecting the sun.

He sat down on the wooden slats of the porch and took the weight off. The horizon looked different than it did just hours before.

CHAPTER 31

He walked over to the window, where Mikaela still stood by the sink, like a mother. Through the window, he said, "Something's building out there. Did you see the horizon?"

"The water is backing up, where the lahar blocked the rivers. A lake is forming. I saw it from the car before." He nodded his head, then he walked around the corner and stared at the horizon again. Water has a way of going where it wants, he thought, like the way it can bore holes in and sculpt rock. Not far away was a brand-new river. At least they *had* a water source.

"Push me," he heard Amy command.

Beatrice came forward, found Amy from behind, gripped each side of the swing, and stepped back carefully, still holding on to the swing.

She gave the swing a gentle push, then stepped back a few more steps, one arm held forward to fend off the back-swing. Amy kicked up her legs, gripped the chains, looked back, smiled.

"Millie and Tom want to swing!"

"Where are they?" Cooper asked.

"Over there!" Both of the smudged and tattered dolls were perched, half seated, against the wooden posts of the porch.

"Here?" Cooper held up the empty swing.

"No there! Silly!"

He walked over, picked up the dolls, and plopped them one on top of the other on the free swing, belly first.

"Give *them* a push. They want to swing!" She was insistent, as usual. Kids had a way of escaping into play. It worked.

Cooper gave the swing a nudge, and it moved awkwardly with the two dolls; "reek...reek."

"What do you miss?" Cooper said. He moved over and leaned against the swing-set's frame. The metal was warm in the sun. It felt good just to prop up his weight.

"Reading," Beatrice said.

"What's your liking?" he asked, thinking *books written in braille?*

"Audio books in the car. I listened to one about the life of George Washington. And books for the sight-impaired; I just read *To Kill A Mockingbird*. I have a copy of *The Bible, King James version*. I'll just pick it up and open it to a section. Yes, I know that sounds old-fashioned."

"No," Cooper said. "I heard there's good reading, great passages in the Bible. Great stories." He hadn't had any religion lately himself; since way back when before his father died. He pondered a distant memory of his father standing behind Shane and tying a necktie, before Cooper knew how to do it himself. Then his mother handing him a really stiff, uncomfortable sport coat, with the tie already strangling him, before they all went off together to a Lutheran church in Vermont. Songbooks and Bibles tucked into the back of wooden pews.

"I miss the radio. I listen to it every morning, in my pickup truck, and even over the Internet." That made him think of a D.J. he liked, on FM radio on the western slope of Colorado. One time the guy got drunk on screwdrivers on air, with a police chief and a fire chief sitting on either side of him, in order to draw attention to impairment while driving. It was the morning before New Year's Eve, and a date he had with Alexis.

"I find the Bible reassuring," Beatrice said.

"Keep pushing, *higher*!" Amy called back, curt and urgent.

"Hold your horses there, you frisky filly."

"What did you call me?" Amy looked back at Cooper, her mouth wide open in a gasp. Beatrice caught the swing and gave it a good shove.

"You know, you're really good at that," Cooper said. "I mean, you can't even see the swing."

"You get this sixth sense, about everything," she said wistfully, without bragging. Cooper thought she'd grown more faculties, ones we don't have, after God took one of hers away.

"What do you think of this house?" Cooper asked, kicking at what was left of the sand bed beneath the swing-set. "Kind of a cozy place, for a time."

She paused a moment, holding the swing still. "It's not a home, in the strict sense of the term. It's a box full of treasures. I wish I could do more. I wish I could search it with a fine tooth comb, like you and Mikaela do."

"I noticed they had a basement. You can go down there with me, kick around a bit, before we leave."

He was impressed that Beatrice already understood the essentials of survival. *Nothing found is useless; nothing is wasted. Scavenge, scavenge, and keep scavenging; you never know when some seemingly useless piece of scrap will prove invaluable, save your life.*

But how were they going to carry the stuff that they find, once they finally leave?

He wandered over to the back of the house, where he'd seen the tipped-over grill and ruined fencing. After a brief inspection, he found, tucked into the home's foundation and under a tarp, a large wooden canoe. At the stern of the canoe was an attachment with small rear wheels.

He removed the tarp, and pulled the bow of the canoe away from the house. He felt like a 90-pound weakling all of a sudden; pulling the canoe was bulky and laborious.

The boat was full of wet leaves. He scooped them out with his hands. He didn't find any rot, yet. The boat still appeared sturdy. Muddy water had collected beneath the leaves.

He unfastened the wheels from the stern of the canoe, set them aside, and with great difficulty, overturned the wooden boat and let out some of the water. He left the boat leaning on its side.

He also found two mountainbikes leaning under the eaves against the foundation. One of them had flat tires; the other had tires about half inflated. Both had rusty chainrings and chains. He pulled the one with viable tires away from the house and wiped the seat off. *Where there are bikes, there are bike-tire pumps*, he thought.

He laid the good bike on the ground next to the boat. He stood up, weary, hungry, and faint, and scanned the eastern horizon through fading daylight. Rainier's gouged-out higher reaches, still partially snow covered, were draped with a cloud which surrounded it like a skirt. Over above the trees, near the floodwaters and where they'd left the car, he saw a column of black smoke snaking into the sky.

CHAPTER 32

They all walked back to where the high water ran roughly over the fringe of the lahar. Dusk had arrived quickly. Cooper carried the crossbow, armed. Beatrice, Mikaela, and Cooper clutched some empty plastic bottles that Mikaela had found and emptied out of rotten or soured contents. They could be washed out and re-used. Even Amy carried one.

It took them more than half an hour to climb back up on the lahar and walk the mile back to the river. The water raged over the debris–higher, faster, and more frothy than before. They walked along its edges for quite some distance, at least 50 meters of ragged ground, until they found a flat area for reaching down and dipping the bottles into the rapids.

"Did you see that blue shimmer, out on the horizon?" Cooper asked. Beatrice stood back with Turk and Amy.

"It's gotten more prominent," Mikaela said.

They both were on hands and knees and holding the open nozzles into the rushing water. The water pressure was so hard it took longer than you'd think to fill a bottle. Most of it spilled over the sides.

"Don't drink it," Cooper said, as much to himself as anyone else. "It must have a lot of contaminants and pollution, from all the crap in the lahar. We're going to have to disinfect it."

The black smoke still rose above the trees. He was glad the water was violent; it was much harder to cross. It was the reason, maybe, why they hadn't encountered Gladys's henchmen again.

They filled the bottles with at least six liters, and by the time they were finished a thick fog had rolled in. It came from the west, toward the coast. He thought he smelled the briny ocean in it. He slung the crossbow over his shoulder and gripped a liter in each hand.

He felt like crap, as if the distance, only a mile plus, back to the house was going to be a slog for him.

Even Amy had to carry a bottle, and when she instantly tipped it up to drink when they handed it to her, they made her spit out the mouthful. They would have to spend the night in the house, Cooper thought, and they could come back in the morning for more water.

The fog was impenetrable. It wrapped around them like a wet blanket. He was afraid that they'd go off course, and if that happened, they'd be spending the night outside. He wished they'd marked the trail. Carrying the bottles, they tracked back to the part of the floodwaters they'd encountered first, where it was steep and dangerous.

He knew the floodwaters ran east-west, and the house was due south from there. *Damn!* He didn't even have the compass, which was in the rucksack, which in his spaced-out condition he'd left in the kitchen.

"Pea soup!" Mikaela declared. She clicked on a flashlight, but it was a fog like smoke; you might as well aim a beam onto a curtain.

They began to follow Mikaela. The sun was blocked and it felt, to Cooper, like it had dropped 20 degrees Fahrenheit. The moist, knobby ground had a sterile sameness, like a desert where nothing grows. There were no landmarks with which they could keep their bearings. It was white-out conditions, and he thought of Arctic explorers stepping out of their tents in a blizzard, losing the lifesaving wands.

"You think you know where you're going?" he called out, then stumbled. He heard, "I think so."

Amy and Beatrice walked hand in hand, with Turk beside them. If someone veered ten feet either way, he thought, they would disappear. He thought they all should be connected by a rope. It had begun to rain, a fine mist. He shivered and watched veils of mist drift in the smoke illuminated by Mikaela's light beam.

He felt engulfed by a viral paranoia. He dropped both his bottles and turned with the crossbow; loud splashing, the crunches of footfalls. He raised the bow and through the scope, he saw a bulky form run toward them in the fog.

CHAPTER 33

Shane centered the man in the cross-hairs of the crossbow's scope.

"Get on your knees, now!" he said gruffly, still feverish and sweating from the forehead. The man knelt down in the fog, both of his hands raised over his head. The fog had thickened. The two of them were suddenly alone. Magnified, Cooper could see a wet man in shirtsleeves.

"What are you doing here? Were you following us?" It would be easy, a release of tension, to let the arrow go. Cooper was getting used to it, the ease of firing.

"I'm on the run! Like you! I gave you water, back at the compound. Remember? I helped you escape!"

"How come I don't recognize you?"

"Let him go, Coop. I know him." It was Beatrice, appearing behind him. "He's the man who helped me. That's you, Lucas, isn't it?" The man began to stand up unsteadily, arms still in the air.

"Yeah, yeah, it's me. Lucas." Lucas wiped the mist and

a bit of blood off his face with the back of his hand. His eyes had a desperate, fearful gape. Cooper lowered the crossbow.

"How did you find us?" he said.

"By accident. I mean, I just made it over those wild waters."

"How?"

"A fallen tree. I crawled over it. Almost dropped in– got killed."

"Are they behind you?"

"Who?"

"Gladys's retard brigade. Aren't you one of them? Because if I find out you're lying to me..."

"I'm not, I swear. I'm on the run. They want me dead, after what I done. I think I lost 'em. They found your car. They siphoned the gas, then set it on fire."

"Cooper, let him go. He's a good man." Beatrice reached out and touched Cooper's arm. Cooper shivered and lowered the bow all the way to the ground. My lips must be blue, he thought. We have to get out of the elements.

"Okay, get going. Walk in front of me. I don't trust you. Sorry, man. I can't afford to."

"Let's go!" he heard Mikaela shout from somewhere in the fog. Cooper motioned with the crossbow, and Lucas shuffled ahead.

They rejoined the others, who'd waited for them a short distance away.

"Are you hurt?" Beatrice asked Lucas.

"Not really–nothing broken."

"How far behind you are they?" Cooper said.

Lucas looked behind him, into the opaque curtain of mist. "Not sure if they went over that river, the flood." They could hear the unseen water rushing, louder. It flows from the east, Cooper thought, where the lahar debris backed up rivers and lakes and made a giant reservoir, whose boundary was only temporary. It's not like it had a shoreline.

"I don't think they'll try too hard. I think you might be in the clear," Lucas muttered as he stumbled along. "I mean,

133

they have more important things to do, than wear themselves out looking for you."

"Like what?"

"Like collecting more food. Moving goods to the coast. Getting out of this Godforsaken place. People like you, laborers…"

"Slaves," Cooper corrected.

"…Are expendable. They can always be replaced."

They hadn't seen the house yet through the dense fog. They weren't even sure they were going in the right direction. Cooper found the water bottles he'd dropped; he thrust one to his lips and guzzled it down.

He knew the water needed to be boiled. They needed a fire. He needed to sit beside it and dry out.

Mikaela strode ahead. The fog rose like swamp vapors. Cooper trusted Mikaela to find her way back to the house;. He felt too sick to be confident in his own sense of direction.

She kept walking with the dog and Amy, then Lucas right behind her.

They couldn't feed Lucas, he thought. A bitter side of him, one drained of the energy required for gratitude, wanted to throw Lucas back out into the night, let him fend for himself. He was dead weight. He hoped he wouldn't have to kill him.

He did help Beatrice escape. He'd propped the exit door open; fled down the hallway with Beatrice, putting his life on the line. He gave Cooper some water, when he was hanging from the pole back there.

He saw Mikaela drop down from a dark plateau and hold out a hand for Amy. Turk stood on top of that hillside of debris; he barked once in recognition of the darkness.

Lucas held out a hand for Beatrice. "We're here!" Mikaela cried out.

CHAPTER 34

The sun had begun to set over the distant sea. They could see it like a lamp light permeating a dirty shade. Cooper collapsed again on the small couch, but not before he'd changed out of his wet clothes. They'd rummaged around upstairs in the house, and he'd found an old paint-stained, University of Oregon, extra-large hooded sweatshirt, plus some blankets. He hung his pants and socks up to dry on the pole of a shower curtain, ate some more Saltines, and fell deep asleep.

After delirious dreams in which he spent a lot of time underwater, deep in the ocean amongst sea creatures, and people he didn't recognize, he rolled off the couch, put the pants back on, and ambled barefoot into the kitchen. He picked the instant coffee off the counter. He opened the kitchen door. A fire roared, just outside, in the darkness. Pots and pans of water lay about. Mikaela and Lucas stood by the fire, supervising the boiling.

"Where's Amy?"

"Sleeping."

"Good."

"How do you feel?"

"Weak as a kitten..." He felt rundown, and fraudulent, as though his sickness had betrayed an essential weakness. The night air was cool, no longer suffused with mist. He smelled a mixture of the rot that rose from the lahar, and the minerals he recalled from the floodwaters. The white noise from the raging waters now filled the darkness beyond the flames.

He walked over to the crackling fire, upwind of the cinders and black flecks of ash, and held his hands out to the warmth. Mikaela and Lucas had broken up some furniture and used it to feed the fire.

"Can I use some of this water?"

"Of course." He poured some grounds into a small tin cup, and filled it with hot water. He found a spoon and stirred it around, then sat down on a stool they'd moved from the kitchen onto what was left of the lawn. The weak coffee revived him, somewhat.

"You guys have been hard at work–good job."

"We thought we should put together a couple of gallons, before we leave," Lucas said. He stood looking into the fire with his hands in his pockets.

Cooper looked at him warily. *So he thinks he's making decisions now.*

"Thanks for helping with Beatrice," he began diplomatically. "Where *did* you come from, anyways? I mean, before you started working for Gladys?"

"I didn't work for her. I was, like you put it, one of the slaves."

"But you had guard duty. That's a responsible position, like they promoted you. You were part of the team. You could have run away any time you wanted to." There was silence, only pops from burning wood and the white noise of water. Cooper realized what was missing, crickets. A lone hawk was the only bird or wildlife he'd seen since they'd narrowly escaped the lahar in the car.

"I had nowhere to go, until you guys showed up."

136

Lucas tossed the splintered leg of a chair into the fire. He was skinny with a dark, unshaven face and awkwardly trimmed black hair. The fear, when Cooper first had him in the scope, had given way to a bleak fatigue. He has to earn my trust, Cooper thought. I have to know he's on our side.

Lucas cleared his throat. Mikaela watched both of them silently.

"I was on holiday here, with my wife, Claire. She was with our son, Ryan. See, at that time we were separated. We weren't *divorced*." He wanted to emphasize that point.

"We're from Bellingham. She drove in with Ryan, to meet me. I told her, I'm going to take him into the mountains. See, he's 10. He likes hiking, canoeing, archery, that kind of stuff. 'Meet me in Sumner and I'll take Ryan for the weekend,' I told her. But I was hoping she'd come along, too. We could give it another chance. Another try. That's what I was thinking.

"So she gets into the van, with me and Ryan. We leave her car in the park n' ride in Sumner. We had lunch outside, on a picnic table in the sun. Sandwiches, ice tea, chips, and cupcakes. We were getting along; Ryan was excited, about hittin' the trails. I can still hear his laugh. It was like the old days. Life is like that sometimes, isn't it? It's good, just purely good. Nothing gets in the way. It sticks in your memory that way.

"We get into the van. We start driving east, towards Rainier National Park. I see that thing coming, the lahar, the first one. I thought it was a local mudslide, a flash flood. Then it just gets bigger, grows in volume. I put the van in reverse and I try to outrun it. Then I know I can't go that fast in reverse, so I pull a U-ee, turn the van around–Ryan's screaming in the back...it catches me broadside..."

Lucas paused, choked up. "I don't even know why I'm telling you this..."

"You don't have to," Cooper said.

"They didn't make it," he said, his eyes glistening in the firelight. "I saw the van, what happened to it. I was standing up on these rocks; I'd had Claire's hand, but it slipped out. Then I walked away. I walked for...I don't know how far. I was a zombie. Then those criminals found me. 'Come with us.' In a weird way, I wanted to do their dirty work, to forget."

"Sorry about your family," Mikaela said.

"Hey listen Lucas, I found some stuff in the backyard here," Cooper said. "I think we can use it. I could use your help with it."

"I worked on maintenance for UPS. I fixed trucks. That was my thing."

CHAPTER 35

They set up the canoe as a storage container on wheels. They were in silent agreement that they could get maybe one more night out of the house. The waters were rising to the north, almost as you watched. Besides, they weren't more than 12 miles from Tacoma and the coast. They could make that, Cooper figured, in two days, at a slow pace.

In the morning, they got to work. Cooper was well enough; he'd slept again, having sweaty, delirious dreams. He woke up and pissed the color of rusty water. He didn't know what was happening to him. He just wanted to gut out the remaining miles, like a worn-out man in an extreme endurance race, and hope that Tacoma or Seattle had a working hospital.

Lucas proved good with his hands. They took the bow of the canoe and fastened it to the rear hub of the mountain bike using a crude, ad hoc harness made up of some wadded up bungee cords, wood, nails, and screws they'd found.

Lucas tightened it up, using only the tools that came with Cooper's Swiss Army knife. They searched everywhere,

139

first outside and then through the equivalent of a back porch, until eventually they found a rusty bike pump. They pumped up the mountain bike's tires until they were rock hard. This effort exhausted Cooper, even though he split it with Lucas.

Then they moved the boiled, disinfected water, in containers, into the stern of the boat. Mikaela had found some trash bags, which they wrapped the rest of the food in. They didn't have much to eat, the left-over peanut butter, powdered milk, beef jerky, stale flour they had to pick the flowerettes of mold out of. The plastic food bags went into the stern, along with clothes, blankets, splintered wood for fires, Millie and Tom, and two books. A John Steinbeck anthology that included *The Grapes of Wrath*, and the *Holy Bible, King James Version.*

Cooper found the Steinbeck choice ironic. They were like the Joads, a threadbare, ramshackle crew headed out across the wasteland. The Bible was Beatrice's choice, primarily.

Everyone agreed that Cooper had contracted some infectious organism or parasite, or he'd been poisoned back at Gladys's; this wasn't the run of the mill flu or sinus infection. With urine the color of diluted root beer, Mikaela posed a kidney infection. Lucas thought it might be malaria; he had a friend that got it in Panama. Whatever it was, there was no medicine save the aspirin and ibuprofen from the med kit, which he used to bring his fever down.

He was desperate to get his weight back; he'd lost 10 pounds over the last few days. He drank as much of the water as he could without being gluttonous or wasteful. The Saltines were gone, but he took in fingerfulls of salt from the caky Morton's container.

He needed to find game, with his crossbow. He needed real food to get well; quality protein. Animal fat, cooked over a fire.

If he was dead weight, he was prepared to stay at the house and let them go on, now that he knew Lucas could split the mountain bike riding, dragging the wheeled canoe behind, with Mikaela.

At about noon, he stood by the swing-set and watched the floodwaters, as Amy swung higher behind him. She was getting by, he thought, on pitiable food scraps, only because she was a kid who didn't know any better.

They'd also found about a quarter can of cocoa that was so old that they had to chip parts of it off with a flat knife, and melt it in water. Mikaela mixed the cocoa with flour, no butter of course, to make a crude kind of cookie. Their last meal had been cookies, dried-out peanut butter, and Saltines. It was prison fare; and a good thing they were moving on.

The clouds and vapors had parted before a pallid sun. Like a rip tide just offshore, tearing into a placid sea, he could see whitewater not a quarter mile away. It had already submerged the woods they'd crossed to get here. It had made its way to the lid of the lahar; he thought it was just a matter of time before it migrated across the lahar's surface, like a puddle along a cement floor.

Lucas sat on the porch nearby. Cooper yelled out, half thinking out loud, "We're going to have to go southwest, not just due west. Avoid these waters."

They'd both found hats; Cooper a camouflaged, wide-brimmed hunter's hat with half the brim crushed to the side; Lucas a Seattle Seahawks cap in the baseball design.

"You want to go hunting with me?" Cooper said. He'd fortified himself minutes ago with cocoa and coffee mixed.

"Sure."

"I figure that flood might be driving animals out of the woods, to this side."

"It's worth a try. Wish I had a rifle."

"You a hunter?"

"Yeah, you bet. Deer and moose and once, black bear."

"I'm not. At least at home."

"Then what are you doing with that crossbow?"

"Sport..."

"And you brought it with you, what, for that climb you were telling me about? Guides don't bring crossbows with them. Not that I'm second-guessing you..."

"It makes me feel ready; secure. It was part of my bug-out gear, if you know what I mean. I always had my kit and my crossbow ready."

"I gotcha. I kept a handgun in the glove compartment."

"Licensed?"

"Sure. Not proud of it, though. Just a sign of the times. I wish there were fewer guns in the world. We'd all be better off. But I'm like you. I like to be ready."

"Let's tell Mikaela we're going."

They told Amy to keep swinging and don't go anywhere, and that Mikaela and Beatrice were in the kitchen. Then they headed on foot north, in pursuit of game, the nearby floodwaters casting mist and spray that stayed up in the air like light rain.

CHAPTER 36

Each night when the sun went down, an inky darkness befell the land. All the electricity in the region was out, except for distant pools of light, mostly a few fires left to burn, in the few places in the valley that weren't buried beneath 30 feet of dried-out slurry. The batteries for the flashlights they were using had died. The fire they lit by the house would die down soon.

As soon as the sun set behind an ocean they could only imagine, the blackness would blanket the earth, the ash plumes blotting out the starlight. You could barely see the hand in front of your face. Lucas and Cooper had to get back to the house before sundown.

Despite the vapors that blotted out the sun, the lahar became parched, rock hard, like a Martian surface. Nothing moved, or appeared alive on it or grew, but them. It seemed laughably difficult to locate any live game on the lahar itself. Yet, they still needed food for the days ahead. The pickings were slim.

The muddy floodwaters raged nearby, filled with tree trunks and limbs and other debris not buried by the lahar itself. At one point they saw a car float by, half submerged on its rooftop.

Hearing only the gritty crunch of their boots, they had consigned themselves to returning empty handed. It was nearly dusk; the horizon glowed a fiery orange, of an incomparable beauty next to the scoured, ugly landscape.

Then they they spotted a profile on the horizon. It was impossible to miss, given that nothing else existed but a flat, empty plateau that rolled on for miles. It was a horse, still as a statue. They both looked at each other silently and walked toward it. Sturdy, chestnut-colored, and saddled, the profile reminded Cooper of an iconic statue or painting he'd seen in one of Telluride's lodges; possibly "Pursued" by an artist named Proctor.

The animal looked like it was purposely built as a statue to honor the glory of the sunset. When they got closer, the horse, which had a bridle in its mouth, glanced at them and nodded its head, as if to say, "Yeah I'm stuck out here like you."

It lifted up its foreleg and pawed the ground, blew air out of its lips, as a kind of warning. "Easy boy," Cooper said. He hadn't much experience with horses, even though he'd been around them a lot at home. He was surrounded by horse women back in Colorado. The reins hung free by the side of the saddle. They'd gotten within about five yards, but the horse walked away from them, then stopped. Wary, not spooked.

"Why don't you stop," Cooper said to Lucas.

"Pretty animal," Lucas said, then he glanced at Cooper's crossbow and looked away with a guilty glint.

Don't you dare, Cooper thought. He wasn't killing this beast for its meat. Not yet; they weren't quite starving to death. Besides, the horse was transportation, if he could catch it.

"Easy...easy," he said, holding out his hand. He crept closer.

"Wish we had an apple, or a fist full of grass," Lucas said from a distance. Not 50 yards away, waves of white and brown water sloshed and bucked along the rocks. The disappearing sun burned titian against the sharp lid of the lahar. The breeze blew through the horse's mane, and Cooper could smell the musky hide; the sweat.

"That-a boy," he said, now nearly at a whisper. The horse's head hadn't moved, but the eyes watched him in a sidelong manner. When Cooper got near enough to reach for the reins, the horse threw its head to the side haughtily and exhaled. Its hoof pawed away awkward clumps of debris-clogged ground.

"Easy boy easy boy, I'm your friend," Cooper cajoled softly. "Where did you come from? All the way out here in the middle of nowhere, without a rider? Must have taken a lot to get where you have got." Then instantly he had a grip on the reins and was petting the soft mane up and down, more friendly cajoling. The horse lifted its hooves in place and a quiver moved through the auburn sheen of its muscles, like a wind through western grass.

"You must be one of them horse whisperer types," Lucas said. "A natural."

"Not really," Cooper said. "Just watch, if I try to ride 'im. We gotta get back, and I hope he'll come."

"Got a veritable zoo now," Lucas said. "A dog and a horse."

The saddle was leather and as sturdy and traditional as the horse. Cooper could at least imagine himself sitting on it, but he didn't want to completely spook the animal.

"Let's get back to the house. It's getting dark. I don't have a clue how he got here, but it makes me think there's another way over that river."

"The river from hell," Lucas said. "The River Styx."

"That's right. The River Styx. The River Stinks."

They walked back along the floodwaters, toward the tiny dot of the shimmering flame. It was still going, by the house. The horse didn't fight the reins as Cooper pulled him

145

gently along. He felt like crap again, and thought of hitting that couch when they got back. First they'd search the horse; there was a saddle pack and a rope hooked onto it.

Only the heavy, clip-clop sound of the hooves, then Lucas said, "Where there's a car, maybe something else has washed up. It follows, I mean, maybe it's worth a chance if junk like cars are washing up." He walked over closer to the river and they ambled along it another 100 yards.

The rushing water got louder and louder, until Cooper couldn't hear what Lucas was yelling, standing beside the temporary shoreline in veils of mineral mist, waving his arms.

CHAPTER 37

The deer head was lodged up against a rock, with the flood funneling on either side of it. The eyes propped open and lifeless. A prominent set of antlers stuck out of the water. Violent rapids poured around the body, up to the shoulders.

Cooper and Lucas stood looking at it a minute; it was tough to get to, but at least they had a rope. Darkness settled in; they could see the dark profile of the house and the small flame about a quarter mile away.

"It's going to be there in the morning," Lucas said.

"We don't know that. We don't know that at all." His stomach growled. "It's a big one, maybe a couple hundred."

"Okay..." Lucas said, determined but not knowing how to do it. He put his foot up on a rock beside the rapids. There were chunks of stones and congealed mudflow around the torrent of water and marooned buck, but no safe way to get to it. One slip up and it was a drowning death.

Cooper knew knots; you have to when you guide people. He got the rope down from the horse, which had lowered its head, sniffing the ground in vain. He felt sorry for the handsome beast. The rope had been coiled professionally and tied at the end. Once again, he wondered after the horse's owner.

He uncoiled the rope, about a three-quarter inch one, and tied one end of it to the saddle horn. He struggled to remember, through the fog of his illness, but then worked the other end into a Honda knot. It felt like hard work. Nevertheless, if that knot didn't work, he had others.

"You're going to have to hold on to these," Cooper said. Lucas took the reins in one hand, and stood off to the side to watch.

Cooper held the slack of the rope in one hand, then spun the loop over his head and hurled it toward the deer's antlers. It fell far short, then it was carried away limply downstream. He reeled it in, shook some of the water out, and tried again, swinging it around like a lasso.

The floodwaters generated its own stiff breeze that caught the knot, as if it was hurled against an invisible wall. It fell back into the water. "Goddammit!" he screamed above the pounding brown surf. He reeled it in and tried a few more times; failure. The horse was getting antsy. It stepped backward and threw its head against the reins.

"I don't know how long I can hold onto this thing," Lucas said, grimacing and wary, nervous with horses. Especially this one, which could just rip the rope out of his hands if it was so inclined.

The deer corpse shifted in the rapids, the gelid eyes staring in a different direction.

"Wait. Hold on. I've got an idea." Cooper fetched his crossbow, removed an arrow, and sat down with the rope in his other hand. He was wasted. *Food*, he thought. *This is good food, no more no less.* He needed the nutrients, craved them, as much as any of them. He bound the rope tightly just above the feathered end, then he armed the bow with the roped arrow. He stood up and took aim at a muscular part that he could completely penetrate.

He needed the arrow to hold. He really wasn't far at all. He aimed for the thick part of the neck that was still above water, then fired. The arrow flew across angry waters and sunk into stiff flesh and hide. *Bingo.* He pulled the rope taut, praying it would hold. "Yeah!" Lucas yelled behind him.

"Okay!" Cooper said, his heart lifting with a marginal victory. He stepped back and took the reins from Lucas. "Let's go!" They started slowly walking with the horse, the rope stiffening above the water and against the saddle. The horse, at about 700 pounds of bone, sinew, and hide, didn't even notice that he was pulling something. Cooper was afraid the rope would break, so he took it slow. Darkness fell on the vacant, treeless grounds like a pitch black downpour.

He led the horse gently toward the tiny flame in the distance. "C'mon boy," he whispered.

Lucas stood by the rapids and watched. Apparently the deer was deeply wedged in a rock; the rope was as tight as a metal cable, the buck's neck stretched and resisted. "There it goes...there it goes!" Cooper heard the other man, but couldn't see him. The rope took off downstream as the body was carried by the flood. He led the horse, inexorably, hardly thinking about the dead, water-logged weight on the other end.

"It's out!" Lucas cried. "It's out!"

Lucas strode over to the carcass and yanked at the head and neck to pull it farther onshore. "Jesus it weighs a fuckin' ton!"

Cooper stopped, began to gather up the slack of the rope, then he rewound that and tied the slack against the saddle horn. Now there was only about ten feet of rope and the buck behind them.

Cooper dropped the reins for a moment, went back to inspect the buck. It was intact. He felt like a wet rag, wavering in the darkness. On his last legs. "Let's drag it back," he said.

CHAPTER 38

The strong, unbelievably savory smell of roasting fat
and meat filled the night. The flames rose around a splintered
chair that they'd taken from the kitchen and used to feed the
fire. They'd draped all four of the recovered buck's legs, the
haunches, plus the organs–liver and kidneys–onto the fire. The
grill and hiss had them all starving. It was like torture, waiting
for it. Except that Mikaela had found an old wine bottle in the
basement.

Beatrice, Mikaela, Lucas, and even Cooper were
handing the bottle around and pouring the wine into old tin
cups. Anything was going to make him feel better, at least for
the moment. His attitude, due to the virus, was devil-may-care;
he was taking it about an hour at a time.

The meat, the wine, and the horse made them feel like
they were more than merely surviving, clinging to life. Beatrice
stood and pet the horse, Amy watching off to the side with
Turk, who'd they'd given one of the deer bones. The horse was
tethered to the swing-set poles, still saddled. They'd given him

some water. They patched together a treat made up of flour, molasses, and crackers, which he chomped down in seconds with his huge incisors. They had no more food for him, but Tacoma was only a day's ride and, Cooper figured, with a little luck, their ordeal would be over.

Using the knife, Mikaela sliced off bits of the roasted meat and passed them around. They quietly and ravenously consumed them by firelight. The wine was a lush, old red with a faded label. Drinking it fueled an illusion that they were safe and could spend several more days at the house, brought on by the comfortable internal glow they felt after a couple of sips. Eat the deer meat; get some sleep. Relax, chill out. It was tempting. Cooper was getting hammered on the equivalent of one glass. The wine was fruity and tasted as strong as brandy.

He was the only one to eat the liver, so far. And the kidneys.

"I never could stand liver," Mikaela said. "It always tasted…"

"Don't say it," Cooper said.

"Pissy, sorry…but I'm glad you're enjoying it."

"Yuck! Liver!" Amy said, coming back to the group and sitting cross-legged, eating a piece of venison that looked like dark turkey meat. She pealed some of the blackened skin off.

"Eat the skin," Lucas said, watching her, like an uncle at a family dinner. "It's good for you."

"No! You can have it," Amy, so sure of her tastes, thrust a piece of the skin straight out to him over the fire, a bed of pulsating coals.

"Well sure, okay captain. I love skin," he said, taking the offering. The air was cool, like sitting by an ocean bonfire in the sea breeze. Cooper wondered whether it was cold spray from the burgeoning floodwaters that made an August night feel like October. The relentless waters flowed out-of-sight, out-of-mind, but only temporarily, because they'd have to think about them hard in the morning.

"Well," he said. "Here's to liver. Liver…I love you. I

151

really do. I feel better already." He raised his glass, drained it. Cooper felt like a wino hanging out under the highway overpass, chewing the fat (literally) with his wino buddies. With the buzz layered on top of the virus, he felt a little bit like everything, anything, but himself.

He kept filling his belly with the meat, liver, and kidneys, which he'd mixed in a tin bowl into a delicious ad hoc stew, including the juices. It beat year-old peanut butter. The effect was uncanny; no headache, no overwhelming fatigue. Just a vagrant, tremulous energy that coursed through his arms and legs.

"Do ya good..." Lucas muttered, refilling his glass.

Amy eyed them with a precocious air of disapproval. "Wine's weird."

Next to her was a glass of powdered milk with a little molasses mixed in.

"Do you like your milk?"

"Birthday cake's better..."

"I agree," Lucas said.

Drinking the wine had given Mikaela a weary, artificial wisdom, some distance from the insanity of the last week.

"I didn't tell you what I found in the saddle bag." She reached down at her feet and held up a bottle with a red bow tied around the lid. The bottle had a wide lid and amber contents; no label. In her other hand was a folded piece of paper. "I was saving it."

"What is it? In the bottle?"

"Just wait a second."

She opened up the letter and read it out loud.

Dear Drake,

If you have the saddle bag out I figured it must be an important ride. More than a gallop with Napoleon through the heather...

"Napoleon!" Beatrice gasped.

"That's the horse's name!" Amy said. "Hey, Napoleon!"

"Shush!"

152

...This is just a small token of my love; I hope you don't take it the wrong way, like a girly thing. I know you love honey and this is the real thing, from some local bees and beekeepers. I figure you can stop along the ride and both you and the steed can enjoy it. We don't see enough of each other, and the years go by so fast–and there are so many distractions, bad things happening around us in the country–for two people to forget what they once had. This is a reminder that you're my honey.

Cancer can't tear us apart, at least not yet. So let's make a date. I'll ride the gelding, you the steed, and we'll aim for beyond the sunset. Forever yours, in love,

Gwen.

"Lovely letter," Beatrice said, standing nearby in the fire's dying light.

"It's sad, and now I feel bad about opening up and reading it," Mikaela said. "I feel like a Peeping Tom. Now we know we should keep an eye out for Drake. He owns the horse."

"What a shame," Beatrice added. "He's out there somewhere. Where, I wonder? You sure you hadn't missed him on the way back?"

"Believe me," Cooper said. "There wasn't a living being on that hardpan out there, for miles." *Everybody out in this shitstorm has a backstory, and left someone behind,* he thought. *There's not a thing I can do about it, or to make it go away.* "It's all buried; trees, buildings, cars, from here to Tacoma. Just lahar, and floodwaters. Can't say what's beyond a few miles; we'll find out soon enough."

"I feel bad about opening up the bottle," Mikaela said, looking at it somewhat regretfully.

It's calories, and lots, Cooper thought, more desperate airs occupying his mind. "When we run into Drake, if we do, we'll repay him with a hundred honey bottles. Meanwhile, we can't turn anything down or throw anything out. Can't afford to."

"Alright. Pass me your cups."

Each cup she held under the lid...

They warmed up some of the powdered milk in a pan over the fire, then added the warm milk to the honey, which sat sweet and viscous at the bottom of each glass. It was a treat beyond imagining, along with the roasted meat, considering the maw that was Cooper's stomach beforehand, the hole at the bottom of the hazy sponge of his brain.

No one said anything right away–complements and adjectives would have been hopelessly inadequate.

"Land of milk and honey," Beatrice murmured, from beneath a blanket she'd tossed around her shoulders, cupping the warm tin cup with both hands.

"Anything but," Lucas whispered. "But it still tastes great. I could drink a gallon of it."

"A thousand thousand thousand gallons," Amy said. "Napoleon wants some!"

"Right," Mikaela said, slapping both thighs and getting to her feet. "Then I hit the sack. I have to. I'm wiped out."

"Here here," Beatrice said.

They poured another cup of the sweet mixture, then with Amy's help, Beatrice held it beneath the horse's snout. Instantly a tongue appeared between thick lips and incisors and sloppily lapped up the honeyed milk. Both Beatrice and Amy laughed as the cup emptied and clattered to the ground.

They followed Mikaela inside, until only Cooper, Lucas, and Turk were left beside a pile of pulsating embers and cooked venison. Lucas reached in, fetched a bone that still had some cooked meat on it, and tossed it to Turk. The dog caught it in his teeth, collapsed onto his haunches with the bone between his front paws, and gnawed on it.

Luca smiled and watched him distantly.

They could hear the water gushing westward in the darkness. The breeze carried its muddy scents.

Lucas picked up his empty cup and the bottle, which still had about two inches of wine.

"Best not to waste this, either. Want some?"

Cooper waved him off, then reconsidered. "Oh, alright." He held his cup out.

"You wouldn't make a man drink alone, right?" Lucas said, pouring the wine. "One time I had the notion to stop altogether."

"Well, did you?"

"Yeah, I went cold turkey for a couple of months."

"Me too, for less time."

"Really?"

"Really."

"Why?"

Cooper shrugged. "No particular reason. Maybe it was because I had too many friends drinking too much beer and whiskey. I didn't want to go where they were going. Fights, DUIs, swearing and cussing out their girlfriends. Drinking as though it wasn't an option."

"I drank thinking it would improve my morale," Lucas said. "When I was having a crap day. When you have a crap day, that's when you *shouldn't* drink."

"Drinking isn't all it's cracked up to be..."

"But the wine sure tastes good night..."

"Damn straight, it does."

"You feeling better?"

"I am, oddly enough. Who woulda thunk it?"

They were quiet awhile. Then they both finished the wine and put their cups on the ground.

"I have to sleep," Cooper said. Lucas nodded, and Cooper stood up and left him by the fire and Turk, who was laying by the fire. When he was inside, Cooper heard Lucas saying something to Turk. Then he heard him crying.

CHAPTER 39

Cooper stood barefoot in the morning sun. He was nearby the ashes of the night, a black and gray stain on the ground. The floodwaters were nearly a miracle to behold; if they weren't so treacherous and fatal. He could hear a tremendous roar, like a waterfall. It was good they were leaving that morning, heading a ways southwest.

He and Mikaela restarted the fire with the last pieces of splintered wood, so they could heat up coffee and leftover food. They were down to a pocketful of matches, one being a paper matchbook he'd found discarded on the back of a shelf inside. It read, Fran's Hideaway Restaurant, which probably existed 30 feet or more beneath an epic dried mud pile, he thought. The matches were already a sad relic to a place that had thrived perhaps two weeks ago.

Mikaela opened the back door, held it for Amy, who clutched both her dolls. They stepped out into the sunshine, a calm breeze amidst the white noise.

"Morning," Cooper said.

156

"Good morning."

Amy looked half asleep, and thoughtful.

"Where are we going today?"

"To the ocean," Cooper said. Then with hope in his tone, "And home after that."

Then Amy said, with the wise bluntness that would emerge from her, "Where's home? For me?"

Mikaela knelt down next to her. "You know we're going to take care of you, don't you?" She hugged her.

"Yes."

Mikaela stood back up. "How do *you* feel?"

"You know, I feel much better. It's uncanny…"

"It's the honey, *honey*," Mikaela said. He'd had a big blob of honey on a soup spoon, before he went to bed. "It's a powerful natural antibiotic."

"That. And sleep. And fresh venison." The harvested deer had been a gift, like the honey. He had some strength back, enough to travel, possibly enough to fight and defend them against whatever roamed the blighted region between the buried valley and the sea.

A mixture of cloud and ash drifted by like torn threads, then beams of sunlight came out and lit up Rainier. The mountain was still bright white but deformed and collapsed around the sides, like a giant sand castle struck by a wave.

Standing in the sunlight, Cooper imagined himself on a beach or a wharf by the Pacific Ocean, full of guarded optimism.

"It's been more than two weeks now since all this started. In one day, at most two, I think we're going to be alright."

Mikaela looked up at him as a flame leapt up from the kindling they had started. One more fire for breakfast; coffee. "Those days that you spent before Amy, and me, it seems so long ago. What happened to you? You never told me about that, beyond losing your friends in a van."

He thought it was good to talk about those memories that had haunted his dreams lately.

157

"I went down to this house. A woman was having a baby. They were on the second floor. I heard her moans; the baby squall, all the way back in the woods. She was alone, upstairs. No one was helping her. There was a man, badly injured, on the first floor. She kept saying, 'Get my husband! Get my husband!' I went out and found him hiding in a barn out back. He was hurt. I guess he'd run away from someone, a gang. But he wasn't *that* hurt. He refused to go to his wife. I said, 'Go help her. Just do it!'

He said 'I can't! Can't you see? Help me! I need help!' He was lying on the floor of the barn, in the dirt. He'd lost his nerve. I guess I had, too. I left them. I left all three of them, including the child. I got out of that town as soon as I could. It was a nightmare, that place. I felt terrible about it. I still do."

"You've been helping all of us ever since," Mikaela said. "Look what you did for Amy. You've done everything you could, and more. You're not Superman. No one is."

They were quiet for moment. Cooper picked up a piece of wood that burned like a torch. He held the flame from the stick against a tin cup to heat some instant coffee.

"We need all this to be over," Mikaela said.

She stood up and crossed her arms. She looked westward, contemplating their path ahead, fretful creases appearing in the corners of her green eyes. She never complained, Cooper thought. She was some kind of pillar of strength. She had a soft side, too.

The lahar looked like the most desolate of deserts. Nothing was on the flat horizon but clouds building over Tacoma and Seattle. They looked like they could be plumes of smoke.

Napoleon stood like a statue by the swing. He shuffled around, snorted once, tossed his head against the reins. "How do you want to do this?" Mikaela said, breaking a silence. "With the bike, the horse...everything."

"What do *you* want to ride, the bike or the horse?"

She hesitated a moment. He was going to give her the choice, but secretly wished for her to say "horse."

"The bike."

"Okay." Cooper wasn't much of a rider, a horseman. But he'd make do.

All the provisions were packed in the canoe under a ripped up old tarp. A space had been kept open for Amy to ride in.

"What about Lucas?" Mikaela said. "He looks strong enough. He could help with the bike."

"He could. He's walking, for now."

Cooper got dressed. He gave the horse another cup of sweetened milk, as much of a peace offering as more meagre food to fuel the beast. Napoleon was going to get antsy without more food in his belly. He made a note to get him at least some more of that old crappy flour. Behind him, Amy, Beatrice, and Lucas munched on some leftovers from the night before, and got ready to leave.

They took it slow. They didn't have much choice except to slog it over the lahar; it had buried almost everything in the Puyallup Valley. The plan to go southwest was scrapped, as the lahar filled everything, and in its implacable destruction, led the way to the coast.

From the saddle, Cooper prayed for the floodwaters to hold off. He could her the thunderous roar, and see the spray soar into the air like a fountain. It was a stormy sea crashing against a rugged coast.

The whole thing, the millions of cubic feet of lakes and rivers that Rainier's eruption had dammed, was cutting loose, he thought. Water has to go somewhere; it finds a way.

He had the old wide-brimmed camouflage hat pulled down tight over his forehead, his crossbow strapped to the saddle, the reins in his right hand. No galloping, at all. Napoleon clip-clopped along, passively for now.

A few yards away from them, Mikaela rode the heavy mountain bike, dragging hundreds of pounds of canoe, provisions, and Amy. She'd shifted the bike into its lowest gears, but she still had to stand up on the peddles and push down laboriously over the scaly, rugged ground.

One time the canoe tipped over and they all had to stop and right it.

Soon enough, they realized that this set-up wasn't going to work, so Amy came out of the canoe and joined Cooper on the back of Napoleon. She sat on the part of the hard-leather saddle that sloped upward; she held Cooper around the waist. She loved it; at least someone was having fun, Cooper thought.

"Giddy-up, horsey!" she cried. "Yee-haw! Go faster! Faster!" She cried, kicking her legs around.

"Be still back there," Cooper said. "Chill out, girl. I don't want to scare Napoleon. You'll spook 'im." He wanted to make the coast by evening. He pictured in his mind expansive beaches and a quiet ocean; a feeling of hopeful safety and relief washed over him.

They quickly put distance between themselves and the tiny white home with the swing-set. From far away, it looked lonely and doomed, like a Depression-era house in a dusty plains. It was just a matter of time before it disappeared under the floodwaters, wiping out any trace that they or anyone else had been there, or used it as a priceless refuge.

They'd gone about four miles, almost two hours, when the horse abruptly stopped, raised his head. Cooper heard a sound like the fluttering of thousands of wings, the scampering of tiny feet. Not far away, across their path, flowed an awful river of gray. The movement shifted grotesquely, like insects clustered on a carcass. He could see a multitude of skinny black tails whipping in the wind.

"Good God," Mikaela exclaimed, stepping off the bike pedals. "Holy Jesus. Everyone stop."

"Hold on to Turk!" Cooper yelled out. Lucas was on foot with the dog, and Beatrice.

"What's *that*?" Amy said, whispering into his ear.

Fucking rats, he thought. *Thousands of 'em. Maybe a million.* "Animals, escaping the floodwaters. Running away to

160

somewhere. Don't pay 'em no mind."

"Animals? What kind of *animals*," she said in his ear. "They look like rats! I'm scared!"

"Just don't pay 'em no mind. No mind at all. They'll be gone soon. Don't worry."

It must have taken them five minutes, but it seemed longer, to swarm across their path, heading south, toward Oregon. Some of them pealed off from the swarm and stood on their hind legs, as if having second thoughts, their noses twitching and testing the air in Cooper's direction. Smaller rivulets of scurrying rats broke off from the main swarm. He held his breath; they couldn't possibly defend themselves against this vermin army, that many of them. The little creatures stood like prairie dogs, watching, then finally fell back on their tiny forepaws and kept running.

It was like watching a freight train go by, waiting for it to endlessly finish. Finally, the dreadful migration had gone. It looked like gray smoke in the distance. They must of come from the cities, Cooper thought.

"Little bastards," Lucas muttered under his breath. "Where're we going, anyways? Do you have a plan?"

"The sea. Tacoma. The lahar heads in that direction."

"Tacoma? And then what?"

"Your guess is as good as mine. Hey, don't give me any shit, okay?" Cooper snapped, looking down on him from the saddle. "Why don't you take a shift on the bike?"

Lucas looked at him and grimaced. "What are you? The ship's captain? Captain fuckin' Bligh?"

"Hey quiet down you two!" Mikaela said. "We're all a little unnerved. Right? I *could* use a break from the bike. What about it, Lucas?"

"Fine enough," he said after a pause.

"Let's have some water...water the horse," Cooper said.

The little caravan kept going in a few minutes, for at least an hour. Cooper figured it was about noon, at least. It felt laborious and humid under the weak, filtered sun. They'd reached the outer edge of Tacoma's metropolitan region. It

161

couldn't be much more than five miles to the coast.

The trail on the lahar tilted up, to a kind of plateau. He urged the horse up the awkward path of the brown-oatmeal like substance, dried to a cement consistency. The horse picked his way tentatively up the rocky incline, and when Cooper got to the top he raised his hand in the air.

He took his foot out of a stirrup and swung his leg over the saddle, stepped down, and led the horse towards the submerged wreckage of a huge fleet of ladder trucks, fire engines, and patrol cars.

CHAPTER 40

It was a metallic graveyard that included the burned hulks of ambulance vans. It looked like it had been bombed and strafed from above.

The lahar had hit them full on. He saw bodies strewn about, men and women who'd leapt from their vehicles at the last second, the time of collision. Some of the trucks were submerged and pointed straight up in the air, almost comically, as if planted by giant children, their tires drooping with muddy gob. Behind them, as far as you could see, were the motionless ruins of a traffic jam, frozen in time but twisted and burned; acres of charred, mangled cars and trucks, pushed up into smoking piles like a vast junkyard.

"What is it?" Beatrice murmured behind him.

"A graveyard, full of emergency units, buried in the lahar," Cooper said, tonelessly. "This is why it's been so quiet, why we haven't seen any rescue squads...They tried, but never made it."

He thought he saw the tail boom and rotor of a

helicopter, protruding from the muck about 300 yards away. The Coast Guard, he thought, trying to pull someone from the wreckage.

The strident crack of a rifle shot broke the stillness.

He saw movement, scurrying. A group of men. Three, four of them. Two of them were wearing thick firefighter's overcoats, hats, and boots, the white paint smeared on their faces, giving them away.

Another shot rang out, ricocheted against metal. Cooper dropped the reins and brought the scope of the crossbow up to his eye. He scanned; saw the men, hiding amongst the wreckage. They'd fanned out in separate directions.

"Get down!" he yelled to the others, swinging the scope to where he'd heard the rifle shots. "Take cover!"

He saw a tall man crouched down with a Winchester repeating rifle propped on the ruined chassis of a patrol car.

Napoleon reared, whinnied, and bolted. Rounds from a discharged handgun whizzed over Cooper's head. He heard Beatrice scream, and turned in time to see Lucas drag a limp Amy behind the burnt shell of another rescue unit.

CHAPTER 41

Cooper watched the horse wander away amid the wreckage, not far from the raging floodwaters. Having no destination, Napoleon stopped, the reins dangling behind him. Cooper ran to the back of the smashed ladder truck. He found both Lucas and Amy lying on the ground.

Lucas held onto his upper shoulder, a small dark blood stain on his shirt. "I took one!" he said with a painful grimace. Amy was helped up unsteadily by Mikaela.

"Is she okay?" Cooper said, standing over the girl. "Hit by anything? Feel any pain?"

"No...pain," she said, staring off into space and still mesmerized, rather than frightened, by the bullets that had whizzed by her head.

He then turned to Lucas, who'd worked himself into a sitting position.

"You look like you just got winged," Cooper said. "You got lucky. We can take care of that."

"She's okay," Mikaela said, pulling Amy to her feet and

165

dusting her off.

Beatrice knelt down beside Lucas.

"How can I help?" she said.

"Press something to the wound; your scarf," Mikaela said. "Here..." She took Beatrice's hand, with the scarf in it, and pressed it down on the right place.

"Wow!" Amy said. "That was close! Where's Millie!"

"In the canoe," Mikaela said. "Are they coming?" she said to Cooper.

"I don't know." He crouched in the shade of the skeletal chassis of a truck, clutching his crossbow.

"Why the fuck are they shooting at us? I mean, what the hell?" he hissed. "As if we didn't have enough to deal with. Mount Rainier erupts. Lahars. Now the maniacs. They fire at will, at anything that moves. Like us." He frenziedly armed the bow with an arrow.

"The maniacs!" Amy pronounced. "Give me a rock! I'll get 'em!"

"Just stay down," Cooper said, half amused.

"What do you want?" Cooper yelled out to their assailants, his head half tilted for the response.

"Is that you? *Numbnut*? I thought it was you!" came the hoarse reply, which sounded half-drunk. "Call off the hero with the rifle and we'll let y'all go."

Cooper recognized the voice of the thug who'd hit him with the butt of his gun, and taken him in the pickup a few days before. It wasn't a fond recognition.

"You're out-gunned pal," Cooper yelled out. Then he glanced at Mikaela and Amy, concerned. "You guys better clear out, find some cover."

A loud exchange of bullets echoed with a twang amidst the metallic ruins–first the rifle, then pops from handguns. *They can't have unlimited ammo,* Cooper thought. *Then again, they have been looting the Walmarts...*

In the near distance, Cooper saw the man crouched down with the Winchester propped on a piece of metal debris. He heard the rifle fire, and when he looked through the scope

166

at the four assailants, who'd taken refuge alongside a pile of empty 55-gallon drums, he saw one body slumped in the dirt.

Two others with white smeared faces took cover behind the barrels, along with the man with the long, greasy hair beneath his camouflage hat.

"Where's Gladys?" Cooper called out, distracting him.

"None of your Goddammed business!"

"She's probably wondering where you guys are. You better get back to mother. Or there's going to be trouble."

"I'm sick of you," the man called out, hoarse and throaty. "I'm going to be done with you."

Cooper stole another glance from the vantage point of his refuge, behind the huge front fender of a half-buried ladder truck. Two of the men had scuttled closer to Cooper's position, including the one he was trash talking with. They appeared to work in tandem, both brandishing handguns. The third guy had disappeared.

The sky was empty and blue, like a cobalt dome that magnified and hollowed out the sound of firing guns. The air carried a hint of cordite and ocean breezes over the deadened land. The liberated waters roared a short distance away.

Cooper armed the bow; he placed it at his feet. Still shielded by the wrecked chassis, he put his hat on a stick and decoyed it overhead. Two more rounds whistled by. The men were getting physically closer. He shooed the others deeper into cover behind the truck carcass, then crept to the other side of the burnt hulk and crawled into a space beneath it.

He had just enough room to slide along on his belly, bow in one hand. He stopped and aimed his bow out the other side, the wooden stock nuzzling his chin. He stared through the scope, just when two more rounds came crashing inside the wheel-well beside where he lay, exploding into sharp fragments and dust.

The fragments felt like glass; they skinned his forearm and smashed the scope on his bow. "Goddammit!" he screamed, enraged, scrambling backwards from beneath the wreckage. He leapt to his feet, the bow at the ready position at his chin. He strode quickly out into the open. Sunlight blasted the area; light brown dust rose into the air. It was silent.

He'd taken both men by surprise. They leapt from their hiding places, just as he triggered the arrow, hearing two rifle shots in quick succession afterward.

The sound of a waterfall's roar filled the air. The arrow, at close range, impaled the man in camouflage, just beneath the clavicle and near the tips of his dark scraggly hair. A hand leapt to his heart and his neck, as though he'd swat at a mosquito, then his fingers found the fletching of the arrow. Dark blood flowed freely around the fingers; his eyes went glassy and the legs collapsed under him.

My Goddamned bow, the scope is broke, Cooper thought, suddenly feeling disarmed and helpless.

The other man was slumped amidst the empty barrels, a handgun dropped on the ground. The third man was, for some reason or other, long gone.

CHAPTER 42

The rifle man came out from behind his barrier and strode toward them.

"You stole my damn horse!"

"We *found* your horse."

"Where?"

"Out in the middle of nowhere, standing there riderless. What would you guess his name was?"

"What do you mean, *What's his name*? Are you testing me? I've been looking for that animal for the last three days, since we got separated. Right, Napoleon, you lazy old grazer. I'm glad to see you anyways."

He had a gray stubble, was slightly stooped in a manner that originated in the hips, yet still wore his frontiersman garb with comfort.

"You must be Drake."

"Yeah. How did you know that?"

"We found a letter, in the saddle bag."

"I can give it to you," Mikaela said, fetching it from a

169

pouch in the canoe.

"C'mere boy!" Drake yelled over to the horse, which stood diffidently at a distance. Above him, the sun reflected a rainbow in a fine mist that rose high above the roiling waters.

Drake pulled his hat down lower over his forehead and clapped his hands. "I shake a feedbag he comes in a second. Not when I call though. Where did you come from?"

"A few miles back. We've been on the run. Found a few homes on the way."

"I can imagine," he said, still distracted by his pursuit of Napoleon, which he found annoying. "I can imagine it, how bad it's been. You get here, all intact? Everybody here?" he said, his eyes falling on Amy.

"We're all here..."

"What's *your* name?" he asked.

"Ruff," she said, without hesitation. "I rode here on the horse, all the way-zee. Almost."

"I'll bet you did," Drake said, smiling. Then with a deceptively quick maneuver he caught the horse and grasped the reins in his left hand. It reared back a bit, almost by habit.

"Yeah," Drake said, looking around at the horizon and the sky, which Cooper had noticed contained, for once, fewer signs of the volcano's fumes. "It won't be long before we're standing in a lake here. Right on this spot. Yup. Time to get moving again."

Mikaela walked up and handed him the letter, which he unfolded and read, still holding the reins.

"We owe you a full bottle of honey," she said.

"Don't worry about that," he waved her off. He looked up after he'd finished the note, with an expression of renewed urgency.

"I have to go *that* way," he said, pointing southwest though the ruins and wreckage. "The waters are coming." They could see the violent froth as heavy rapids are visible from a boat. "This area will fill up quickly, as a floodplain. It won't be pretty. You better move fast, the same direction I'm going in."

"I have to get to my wife," he added, slipping a boot into a stirrup and hauling himself heavily up onto Napoleon's saddle. He'd slung his rifle into a leather sleeve that was attached there.

Cooper scanned the neighborhood warily; maybe all of the men were gone now. Maybe.

"Have you been dealing with those guys long? Before we got here?"

"You mean the mangy vultures? No. Just came upon them, stripping the bodies of the firefighters. So I fired a few shots over their heads, like I would for the buzzards. Shoulda' just shot 'em right off. Before I know it, I'm in a firefight. There's looting all over this part of Tacoma, owing to what happened to the rescue folk, and the police."

Cooper looked at the boat, the mountain bike, and Mikaela. He wondered what she was thinking, about the next step they had to take.

"Do you know how far the lahar stretches?" he asked.

"It stops about a half mile from this spot," Drake said. He leaned on the saddle horn. "There's no electricity, no gasoline, no open stores, at least when I came through last. Then you get closer to the coast, which isn't more than a few miles, and things begin to get sorted out."

Drake gazed off from the saddle with an impatient air, fringed with guilt. The wind blew through scraps of stray wreckage. The immediate area looked like a battlefield, strewn with the fallen.

"That boat of yours," Drake said. "How many...?"

"Three," Cooper said. "Amy, Mikaela, and Beatrice."

"Now wait a minute," Mikaela said.

"We can walk," Cooper said, referring to him and Lucas. "Or swim. Or we'll find another boat."

"No," Mikaela said, firmly. "We're all going together. We're not splitting up. Not after what we've been through."

"I'll go," Lucas said, standing up and brushing the dust off his trousers. He had a bandage taped to his arm. "Now. Before it's too late. I came late to the game, if you know what I

171

mean. I'll head in *that* direction, southwest, where Drake's going. Before those waters rise. It'll get out of hand. I thank you for your help. It can't be that far, right?"

"The port can't be much more than four miles from here, as a crow flies," Drake said. "Maybe less."

"Good luck." Cooper stepped forward and shook Lucas's hand. Lucas turned and walked away, then he turned back to look at the group. "Bye Ruff," he said.

"Bye Lucas," Amy called out, with a cheer the others could not muster. "We'll see ya on the other side!"

Lucas smiled, "See ya on the other side." Then he wandered with a slightly gimpy gait into the ruins, holding his arm.

"I'll try to keep an eye on him," Drake said. "As far as Tacoma and the port."

Beatrice came forward, without glasses, which had been lost in the chaos. Her eyes gleamed in their visionary manner.

"Napoleon, doesn't he have room for one more?"

"Beatrice..." Mikaela said, yet not resisting.

Drake looked backwards at his saddle, in a friendly, conciliatory way. "Well, you're a petite lady, so I'd say yes, we have room for you on the saddle back there. Right Napoleon?"

He stepped down from the horse. Beatrice offered her hand, and smiled, more at the horizon. Drake took it.

"Are you blind m'am?" he said.

"Yes. Give me a moment." She turned to the others and held out both hands. "Please take them," she said. Amy took one hand and Mikaela the other; Cooper joined them and they formed a circle.

"I'm grateful that you rescued me and kept me safe. Forever ever grateful. I know you'll make it to safety, to the sea. I just know it. We'll be together again, some day." Her words rang true and eloquent on that barren plain.

She then hugged them all, an especially long one for Amy, then stepped to the saddle, to be helped up there by Drake. Then he hefted himself onto the horse's back.

172

"You got enough food, and water, for today?" he said, steadying the horse with Beatrice clinging to his waste.

"Yeah."

"And you have the boat..."

"Better get going now," Cooper said. "Thanks again for helping Bea."

Drake tipped his hat, then made a clicking sound with his tongue. He pulled on the reins. They watched the two riders and Napoleon make their way through the burned out chassis and wreckage, until they couldn't see them anymore.

CHAPTER 43

Soon, the water was around all of their feet. It had risen to the lahar's lid, and now it was migrating in a way Cooper knew would get bad. It reminded him of a basement flooding on concrete.

They had the boat ready, removing everything that didn't need to be there. Just before they were going to board, a van drove up and skidded to a stop. The water was still about puddle depth. Cooper sensed a sickening catch in his throat. Two men piled out with a quickness to their motion, then an old lady stepped down from the passenger side. She had black wading boots on. In her hand, she carried a pair of sneakers.

"Hey there Cooper," she said, as they wandered up. She looked around, disapprovingly.

"Wow, what a mess. Things just keep getting worse and worse, don't they? Then I hear that my boys spotted you, and that you were shooting at them."

"They shot first."

"That's not what I heard. I heard about a fellow on a

horse who started the shooting. Well, he seems gone for now. No horses around here, don't blame 'em. We'll find him soon enough. Shooting...tch-tch...what is this place coming to?"

One of the men went and checked over the two bodies nearby, one shot by Cooper, the other Drake. The third body was about 10 yards away, but he didn't seem to notice that one. Then he looked up at Gladys and said, "They're both dead."

"Good heavens."

The water had risen to their ankles now.

The crossbow was stowed in the middle of the boat. Cooper felt around in his pockets for the army knife, but that too was stored away. Amy was already sitting in the middle of the boat, with Turk.

"I can't just *let it go,*" Gladys began to explain, in her facetious tone. "Behavior has consequences, right? What would that say about me, the way I do business, if I just let it go, every time someone decides to attack us? One thing leads to another, then all the respect, *poof,* up in smoke." Two of the men drew machetes. The water rushed loudly, almost deafening, just over a rise.

Mikaela stepped forward. "You're going to have to go through me, first."

"And me," Cooper said. The men made a motion forwards.

"Don't do it!" Amy cried out, her chin quivering and her mouth drooped downwards. "We didn't do anything to you! We didn't! I don't want to be alone again, me and Turk! Please! Don't do it!"

"Wait," Gladys said. The men stopped in their tracks; one of them with a confused scowl.

"What's your name?" Gladys said.

"Amy!"

"Is this your daddy?"

"He might as well be!" Amy said, tears streaming down her cheeks.

"What about this lady here, is she Mummy?"

"She's just like Mummy!"

175

Gladys paused for the moment, and all they heard was the torrent in the air, the trickling and flow of floodwaters around their ankles. Amy's sobs.

Mikaela, Cooper, and the two men stood there like statues. Then Gladys said, "Let 'em go. Let's get out of here. The water's getting deep."

"You sure?" one of the men said, with a sneer.

"Git!" she said. "Back to the van." The two men turned and began to splash back toward the vehicle.

Gladys went to go, then she turned back to them. "Amy, you take care. You hear? Take care in the boat. Do what they say, and you'll be alright." Then she walked back to the van, got in, closed the passenger door behind her, and it started up and skidded away into the flooding ruins.

CHAPTER 44

They had an old wooden paddle they'd found back at the home. Mikaela was in the bow, Cooper in the stern, Amy huddled with Turk in the middle. Everything else that wasn't needed immediately was discarded.

It didn't take long for the water to rise enough to lift the boat. Soon, it flowed in small waves, like a tide coming in over a mudflats. They were forced to stand by the boat, until the depth was enough to hold all of them.

Cooper got in last. He stepped into the back of the boat and shoved off. They didn't have much choice but to go with the current, which carried them south to southwest through the wreckage of the buried traffic, then the city outskirts.

Cooper steered, but he often had to hand the paddle to Mikaela so that she could use it to fend off various obstacles the water would take them into: the hulks of cars and trucks, floating debris like tires and refuse cans; utility poles and partially submerged fences, even the foundations of buildings.

177

Cooper considered waiting and climbing to higher ground. For the night. But he didn't want the water to rise so high that it would be too dangerous to move, even in the boat.

First the wavelets came, as the floodwaters broke for good over the edge of the lahar. Then the water rose with a deceptive speed. They'd scrape bottom here and there, such as on a submerged curb, when suddenly they'd float past a parking meter, with only the meter showing above water.

The surface of the water glistened with multi-colored gas and oil slicks. The sun began to go down. They did their best to steer past the forest of smashed cars, which waves now lapped up against, and into what seemed like wider spaces and underwater streets between the buildings.

But they had to go where the powerful floodwaters wanted them to go.

They saw the silhouettes of people on the roofs of buildings, but no lights as the sun dipped for good behind floodwaters and ocean.

"I'm *scared*," Amy said. "It's getting dark. I don't want to be in the boat when it's dark!"

"Just pet Turk," Mikaela said. "Turk likes your company." The way the water covered everything, and enclosed the shadows, and its sound, the gurgle and splash, reminded Mikaela of Missy, and that night of looking for her in the dark pond. Especially as night fell.

It was like floating through a city via its harbor, but everything was too close. Shop windows, brick facades with black-iron grating; signs with silly messages made even more meaningless by being partially submerged. Chainlink fences that were supposed to be surrounding lots, spaces that were now fetid pools of black water in the dying light.

They floated through it all silently. One of the things Cooper feared but didn't talk about, because they really couldn't do anything about it, was the flood's magnitude. He feared that it would be as violent as the lahars themselves; suddenly appearing as a monstrous wall or jet of water that would wash them all away to oblivion. But it wasn't, so far. It was just steadily rising and spreading water.

If you left a hose going on a black-top, he thought, the water would jet out of the nozzle with force, but then it would spread calmly along the wider area of the pavement. That's what it was like.

"Tell me a story," Amy whispered. They were now floating in an inky blackness. Mikaela was nodding off in front; they both were. Cooper began to haltingly talk about a canoe trip he took once on the Charles River in Boston. He hoped that they were floating in the right direction, and that sometime around midnight, they'd run aground in the part of the city that was still functioning.

"We were floating in a canoe in the dark, like this. But we were surrounded by the lights of the city." He could see some lights twinkling now, in the distance toward the ocean. "There was music playing. There was a concert on the shore."

"What kind of music?" Amy said.

"It was classical music, the *1812 Overture*. That was it. A huge crowd watching music at a venue they called the Hatch Shell. Tens of thousands of people, and we're floating past this massive crowd. All the lights shined on the stage, and reflected across the water."

"The 1812...?"

"Yeah, it goes..." And then he began a lame attempt at reproducing the *Overture*. "Bah-bah-bah-bah bah-bah bah-bah bah bah Boom! They fired cannons between the refrain. Then fireworks went up..." His voice seemed too loud over the trickling water.

"How many people were in the boat?"

"It was crowded, like this one." Mikaela passed some food forward, the ad hoc, old-flour based cookies she'd made. She dipped them in honey; Drake was nice enough to leave the bottle with them. They had to pay Drake back some day, Mikaela had thought. She wondered whether they'd ever see him or Beatrice again, and she had an image in her head of the horse galloping, with both of them in the saddle, trying to escape the rising waters.

179

Even Turk got some cookie. Once in a while, he'd fidget; Cooper would hear his claws scraping along the bottom of the canoe. It was like he wanted to jump out of the boat after smelling something in the dark. He'd issue the type of light, throaty bark that involved air puffing out his cheeks, and Amy would put her hand on him and he would calm down.

Cooper thought of the beers they passed around the boat that night in Boston. A brown-paper bag full of cold cans. There was a girl he was sweet on, but she was sitting next to another guy. What was her name? *Robin,* that was it. *Pretty face; long brown hair.* He'd jumped overboard and swam beside the canoe in the choppy, tepid Charles River, just to get her attention.

"Bah-bah-bah-bah bah-bah bah-bah bah bah Boom!" he sang again. He thought of the fireworks that night, like confetti someone had let go from a balloon. Like tears dripping from stars. He could see some stars above them; the moon began to rise. It cast a four-story building they paddled past into shadow.

"Do you see the moon Amy?" he said. She was asleep in front of him, with her head on Turk's ribcage. It went up and down with the dog's breathing, Amy's long hair bunched up against him, and still as fine seagrass in a windless evening.

He was glad she was asleep. He had a great vision of her waking up, and the boat is by a dock or a beach. He thought of Alexis back in Colorado, and he wondered whether she thought he was dead.

CHAPTER 45

The luminous moon was so bright he could see terrain
in it; valleys and buttes. Like in Colorado, but the Colorado
plains had more colors in them than the moon, that was for
sure.

"Do you see the moon?" he whispered to Mikaela. He
hadn't heard anything from her in several minutes. He talked
to the back of her head, with the cap pulled down.

"Yeah," she said finally. Wearily. "How far do you
think we have to go?"

"Not far. It must be close to midnight." He dipped his
paddle in and moved them forward. The water was as black as
night. It felt heavy, like molasses; like the molasses they poured
in their milk, back then. He heard the trickling, then the faint
noise of sirens carried over the water from far away.

He hoped to God he wasn't paddling in circles.

They decided that when Amy woke up, if she did,
they'd pull over and tie up somewhere. At the very least, they
could stand up and change positions in the boat. They were

stiff and exhausted.

Within half an hour, he steered them into a kind of alleyway, because he saw an open ledge that they could get up on. The main current took them down a wide street—he could picture a city avenue; now it was completely flooded with at least six feet of water. He paddled hard on his left, and he got them up against the stone foundation of a building, where the street intersected with the alley.

He used the paddle to hook the corner of the building and force the canoe into the alley, then they bumped up against a ledge that they could boost themselves up on. It was a building under construction. It was windowless and had dark, empty, unfinished rooms. He stopped the canoe. The building had metal scaffolding built against the facade. He tied the boat with a short tie line to a metal pole on the scaffold.

Amy woke up.

"Where are we?"

"We're going to get out here. Stretch, get a rest. We all need to move, including Turk. Don't go into the water."

"Why?"

"The water is probably dirty. Among other things."

Mikaela got out first, then she pulled Amy up. Cooper held the boat steady by holding onto the scaffolding. Turk sat in the bottom of the boat watching Amy scramble up to the cement floor.

"Now you Turk," Cooper said. "Go on, boy." Cooper helped him get his paws up on the ledge, then Mikaela hauled him up the rest of the way. The dog stood rigidly, sniffing into the dark space. It was like an underground room, off of a subway. Pitch black.

It smelled like concrete dust, and piss, as if refugees or homeless people like them had been marooned there for a period.

"Anyone here?" Cooper cried into the darkness, his voice echoing hollowly. Nothing in response. They pulled a couple of blankets out of the boat, and food. Cooper made sure the knot was tight around the scaffold. The canoe lay quietly in the water, nudging up against the ledge.

They all stretched out their legs then sat down and ate the remaining cookies and leftover, dried-out venison.

Cooper watched the water flow past beneath them. It can't be more than an hour to the coastline, somewhere around the Port of Tacoma, he figured. Just one more stretch.

About 18 inches more in height and the floodwaters would flood the room, but they didn't seem to be rising yet.

"I'm going to check out this building," Cooper said. "I might be able to see something. I'll be right back. Turk can come with me."

"Be careful," Mikaela said.

He had no remaining light sources so he walked slowly across the room, clutching his bow. His boots crunched on graveled bits of concrete, broken plaster, and probably glass. "Anyone here?" he called out again, louder. Nothing.

Turk wandered along beside him. The first thing he saw seemed like a slumped body in the shadows, or person sleeping against the wall, but it was only a ratty old coat and pair of boots, assorted garbage, and a soggy cardboard box. Turk stopped; his ears tensed.

They heard a sudden and massive scurrying and scratching in the walls; one side of the room to the other. *Fucking rats...here too...*Cooper muttered to himself. "Well Turk, we can't stay here long," he said.

"What?" he heard Amy call across the room.

"Nothing. We won't be long."

They reached a stairwell. It gave off a weak light. The room stank more the deeper they walked into it, and the stairs were dank and dusty. Still, he wanted to explore where they went. From the other side of the wall, they heard the rapid fluttering sound he remembered from the rat swarm; the odd reminder of wings beating, when he knew they were only hundreds of little feet.

They went up the stairs, his shoes crunching on the steps. He decided to arm the crossbow with one of the few arrows he had left. He hoped there wasn't much glass; he didn't want Turk to cut his paws.

They got to the second floor; he opened the door and called in. Nothing but a hollow echo in the darkness. There was at least one more floor. "Mikaela!" he called back down.

"What Coop!"

"What?" he heard Amy's plaintive reply.

"Just checking! We'll be right back." He reached down and gave Turk a reassuring pet. They reached the end of the stairwell. There was a door to the outside, the rooftop; he figured it was locked, but the knob turned freely and the door opened to the night air.

They went outside. "Be careful Turk. Just stay right beside me." It was an open rooftop with nothing but a few HVAC units and a tarred surface. It was bathed in starlight, and he could see many lights in the distance, to the west.

A city was awake, electricity was on, and there was a vibrancy and life on the horizon.

CHAPTER 46

"Do you see that Turk? That's Tacoma. That's the coast. The lights are on. This is where we're going. We'll be in the clear soon."

He saw red lights traversing the sky, miles away. "Helicopters...if we can get their attention...maybe light a fire." Someone else had. About 20 blocks west he saw a rooftop fire. The flames licked and pulsated at a bonfire height. People mingled around it, dancing shadows. Oddly, given the circumstances, it looked like a party. It appeared like they were performing some kind of ritual dance. Maybe it was the Rescue Dance, the Save Me Dance, he thought. The helicopters would see them; surely those red lights were helicopters.

But he didn't have any matches or way to make a fire. He figured they could float 20 blocks from here, or less. It could be less. That's not difficult, from where they were now. It seemed like that's all it would take. He looked down and Turk was sampling the air with his nose, in the rigid, dignified way he did that; the wind ruffling his fur.

185

The breeze was refreshing; it felt great to be high up and in a breeze. The wind didn't carry any of the grit in it. The mountain must be quiet now. He looked back to the east; he saw the Rainier silhouette, a giant gouged-out, luminous shadow.

Everything else in an easterly direction was dark and lifeless. He decided to only look west, from now on.

They went back down the steps and returned to Mikaela and Amy.

"We saw lights!" he said excitedly. "From the roof! All the city lights. And helicopters, the red lights of helicopters!"

"Oh good," Mikaela said, her voice carrying a burden of what they still had to do, to get to the helicopter, if one would come for them. "Should we stay here and wait?"

"I want to ride in a helicopter!" Amy said.

"We could stay on the roof, right. Wait for the sun to come up. But if I'm wrong, about the choppers, then we're stuck here, with the flood coming up. We could paddle the blocks in maybe, half an hour..."

"It's up to you," Mikaela said. She seemed used up.

"I'll paddle us, down that avenue," he said after thinking about it. "It may only take minutes. They probably have a crowd down there, and they're pulling people out of the flooded areas."

"If we're going to go, we should go," Mikaela said. "This place is a little gross. I thought I heard..."

"I know."

Amy held up her dolls, so they could converse. "Are we gonna go now, Millie? Are we going home now? I don't like this place! It's dark, and it stinks!"

"Don't worry, Tom!" the other doll said. "Cooper will protect us. He always does. We're leaving right now! We'll be home soon! Now don't you worry, silly bean!"

"Oh okay, I believe you. Bye, dark place! We're going into the boat now."

"Me first," Cooper said.

He found the commonplace, sing-song tone reassuring,

186

as if Amy knew something he didn't. She stood up. Turk came over and sat down next to her and she scratched behind his ear.

Amy looked up. "Do you think Bea and Napoleon made it out? Oh, I hope Bea and Napoleon are okay!"

"Yup, Beatrice is in good hands," Mikaela said.

CHAPTER 47

They shoved off, and Cooper pushed them off the wall into the wider floodwater stream. The waters moved fast along what he'd thought was an avenue. Too fast; he had a sudden sinking feeling, as if he'd made the wrong decision to leave. All he had to do was steer with the paddle. The floodwaters had picked up. The people moved swiftly through the night.

He saw nothing else around them in the water, but starlit glints. The water fanned and rippled on the surface, betraying the flood current below. The buildings were like stolid, unlit monuments. He wondered where the other boats were. It made him think of the Charles River that time, with the *1812 Overture* playing by the riverbank. The river, then, was a giant flotilla of everything from pitiable little row boats and canoes, to swanky schooners and yachts. Now, there was nothing but their canoe.

They heard a splashing. Cooper saw a form moving in the darkness, not far and coming alongside them. From the form came a desperate panting. The momentum of the heavy, powerful physique beneath the water moved the horse's head back and forth. It drove through the water, overtaking the canoe.

"Jesus," Mikaela said. "Poor horse!"

"Napoleon! Is it Napoleon?" Amy cried.

Cooper could just see the gleam of the eye on the side of the horse's head, which was nearly jet black.

"No, I don't think so. That's not Napoleon. It looks like a black horse."

The horse kept swimming hard. Cooper steered the boat away so it wouldn't upend them. The canoe ran along swiftly in the black water, with a speed that unnerved him. Amy was whimpering, and Turk was riveted and paid attention to the heavy-breathing noise. The strenuous bobbing head of the horse.

Then the horse made its way in the water behind them and was gone, more like a large piece of debris carried away in the flood. They could still hear the forceful panting carried over the water, then no longer, as if the horse had turned onto a side street.

"I hope its okay," Mikaela said. "I hope he makes it."

"Me too!" Amy cried softly.

"I think he'll be alright," Cooper said. "They're good swimmers. A horse can swim pretty well, then it'll be rescued. Pulled out." He was thinking of themselves, too.

It had to be 2 a.m., perhaps later. They floated quickly past buildings. Once again, Mikaela used the paddle from the front to fend off obstacles, as the water swirled around hard objects in their path; trash receptacles and delivery boxes and ad-related newsstands, all of the smaller structures that were embedded in cement in a flooded city and could impede them.

Then Cooper heard a motor behind them. It was unmistakable.

"Do you hear that?" He looked behind them. He saw nothing but black water and starlit ripples. The sound got louder. Then he saw a tiny red light moving about. It was behind them, he guessed 10 or 15 blocks away.

"What is it?" Amy said. She'd been sleeping and he hadn't heard much from her.

"It's a boat. I know it. It's coming up behind us."

Mikaela swiveled around with the paddle in her hand and looked intently. She handed him the paddle.

"The light is getting bigger," she said. "Maybe you should paddle us more over to the side. It's on the water. The light. They have to see us!" She had a hopeful tone, explicitly, Cooper thought for the first time in the last few crazy days.

In a low register, the motor got louder and louder, piercing the silence that had enveloped them, resounding off the concrete walls. He paddled, more frantically. He stroked hard to his left, but they were carried up strongly on top of the current. They were caught up in some kind of swift channel that took them down the center of the avenue.

Cooper could see the strobe light of the watercraft illuminate the building facades as it got closer. A deep wake jetted from both the starboard and the port. The motor was loud now, louder than their voices. It happened very fast. He couldn't steer the canoe laterally as fast as he wanted to.

Mikaela frantically waved her arms in front of him, trying to get the boat's attention. He still held the paddle, then he saw both her, Amy, and the dog bathed in red light. The motor was deafening; the boat wasn't slowing down.

Cooper leapt off the canoe with the tie-line in his hand and kicked and sprinted with his free arm to pull the boat out of the path of the motor boat. The wake hit him hard in the face and he swallowed and choked on the water and he saw over the water's surface the waves hit the side of the canoe as the bright, piercing light swept the street. He heard Amy's scream amid the deafening outboard motors, then the tie-line slipped from his grasp and he went under.

CHAPTER 48

When he came up, the canoe was gone. He moved swiftly through the water. He could see the lights of the boat receding in the distance, and could hear the high-pitched, revved-up whine of its motor. He coughed and kept himself on the surface of the water, which was like a hard-running rapids. He desperately scanned the water surface for signs of the upended canoe, but saw nothing but flood, which was like a large, black moving floor.

The leftover turbulence from the boat, which caused him to swallow more water, subsided. He coughed, spit out the brackish water, fought to breath and stay on the water's surface. He cried out, "Mikaela! Amy!"

It was everything he could do just to tread water. He kept swiveling around on the agitated surface. He felt overwhelming grief, layered with guilt; it was like his own floodwaters welling up inside him.

"Amy! Mikaela!" he yelled out. His voice sounded strange to his ears, sad and desperate. The buildings were going by quickly. He began to swim and stroke a crawl to his left. He made a little bit of progress. He scanned the still-dark area for a place he could pull himself out, but it was no good.

In minutes, ahead of him, he saw a bridge over the avenue. The water height was fairly high up on the superstructure and pylons for the bridge. He thought if he could get over to the side far enough, he could reach up and grab part of the structure, like the edge of a girder. But the bridge came up too fast and he swam hard laterally and missed it. Soon he was well past the bridge with the warped sensation of going downhill in water in the darkness.

The flood had become a kind of waterfall. He was conscious of the chance of being driven into underwater structures and breaking bones and being crushed and drowning, at the same time as he thought about Amy, Mikaela, and Turk. He'd kept looking for the canoe all around, as he was shunted through the floodwaters and fought to stay on the surface.

Another bridge came up in his vision, perhaps two blocks away. He was floating west; light began to leak into the city, and across the waters. He was faintly conscious of the sun coming up, like a shade being partially drawn up on everything.

This time he was about ten feet closer to the edge, and he went for it. It was an all-out sprint as the second bridge approached. A bit of the structure hung down close to the water surface. He thought of distressing videos he'd watched of people trapped in floods, the water brown and just their heads showing.

He reached up with his right arm, timing it just so, and he grabbed a metal pipe as he passed beneath it. He swung his other hand around and snagged the pipe, as his legs were being swept downstream. Water pressure flowed and pulled all around him. Now he was in a pull-up position. His legs still dangled below. But he pulled himself up to his chest and swung a leg around the pipe.

Finally, he was breathless and completely out of the

water, which flew by beneath him. His heart pounded almost through his chest; he coughed convulsively and started to laugh, with a brief instantaneous joy.

CHAPTER 49

He lay on the pipes and rested for he didn't know how long. Then he started climbing.

It was hand over hand with holds to grasp, not like rock-wall climbing, which he had some experience with. He took his time. He got higher on the bridge. He could see the whole route they had taken in the canoe, and thought he saw the building they'd paused in.

It was easier climbing as the light blossomed. Just like with rocks, he made sure he had a firm hold at all times with at least one foot and hand. He looked above him and saw a fairly complex maze of girders.

He was pretty sure there was a road, at least a sidewalk, along the top of the bridge. There was going to be a hard part just beneath the top, a complicated, tough problem. He might have to be hanging upside down; he looked at it a few times and thought about how he'd do it. Then he looked around, and Tacoma's skyline emerged, sunlight glancing off a few taller buildings. The sky was dark blue and stained brown in places as it lit up.

He began to feel the exertion of the climb, a kind of exhaustion that hung outside himself. It made him feel fragile; he cried quietly, in mourning. He thought of the peril the others have been in, and were in. As he hung there and looked for other holds, he watched the water below, swollen, black, and ugly.

He thought he'd done well to get out of it; that was a good move with the pipe and the strength of his upper body and his will to pull himself out of the damned, hellish water. Yet, it had all been ruined because he'd lost the others. A part of him wanted to just let go. Drop back in, close his eyes. That can be good, sometimes, he reasoned, picturing the scenes of their suffering over the past weeks.

You're mad, he thought to himself. You're descending into a silly madness. Just finish this. Just finish this piece in front of you, this climb. Finish what you started, then you can think about more personal suffering and guilty self torture.

He kept climbing. The rust from the girders and pipes was all over his hands; he was already forming callouses. Then suddenly the sun was in his eyes; it was fully up. The light warmed his face, his upper body. He paused with his hands on the metal. He could see Rainier in blazing sunlight when he looked east, and it was still a mountain.

CHAPTER 50

He was just beneath a metal lattice-work that had a railing above it. He reached up, and it was one big move using only his arms. He has no business making this move, and winning it, he thought. He has nothing left in his arms; the muscles have tanked.

The floodwaters churned below, breaking up against the bridge's pylons.

Then he was hanging by his arms and his legs dangled and he hooked a leg up and into the lattice-work, with the toe of his soggy shoe. Then he had an arm over the railing and he flung himself over and onto the road.

He lay on the road on his back, bruised, soaked, tired, and aching. Even though it was pavement, it felt good, as though he'd been poured on it.

Nothing came down the road. The sun was bright; it made vivid red and yellow spots behind his eyelids. Then he opened his eyes and forced himself into a sitting position, and on to his feet.

He began to trudge down the middle of the road. It was empty, pot-holed, and dusty, with a vacancy suggesting disuse. From his vantage point on the bridge, he watched the floodwaters drain westward through the abandoned city blocks. The rooftops were empty, the buildings were dark. A black loneliness swept through him, as if Shane, for so long the loner's loner, could never tolerate being alone again.

He recalled a mountain-guide friend's comment once, weary of his affluent clients, that "people aren't tough anymore."

"Well I'm tough," Cooper said out loud, still walking, a staggering swagger. "Mikaela's tough. And Amy's tough, too."

He saw a vehicle coming down the road, from a mile away. It had a rotating red light on it. The van quickly came closer, raising some dust. He stood in the middle of the road and waved his arms over his head.

He rode in the back, with the EMTs. They took him to the Port of Tacoma, where thousands of people had gathered; the missing, and the people searching for the missing. The flood played itself out; the brackish water poured into the port and continued out into the Pacific Ocean.

An EMT in the vehicle checked out his vitals. She gave him a liter of electrolyte drink, two ibuprofens and a handful for the road, as well as a protein bar. She carefully patched up several scabbed and irritated punctures and bruises. To Cooper, she radiated trust, kindness, professionalism.

"Where are you from?" he said.

"Originally? Costa Rica."

"What's your name?"

"Consuela," she said. "Yours?"

"Cooper."

"You're not in bad shape, Cooper. Considering." He nodded.

He asked them if they'd seen a canoe with a lady, a young girl, and a dog, but they said no and he could inquire after them at the Port of Tacoma. Consuela was so kind and together, he thought, that she appeared to single-handedly restore his confidence in official order, but he figured that this was partly, or mostly, because of his exhaustion.

They arrived at the port, and while there was some kind of agency task force manned by various uniformed personnel, it was mostly the Red Cross. He recognized the tents. Hundreds, thousands of people were milling around. Vacant-eyed, bedraggled like him; some having intense conversations. He wasn't used to crowds; it seemed months he'd wandered the wasteland. Someday, he vowed, he'd piece together the whole thing; how many hours he'd spent in Rainier's devastating shadow.

When he went outside, he immediately saw a long row of dark green body bags, tagged and laid out on the tarmac. He went over to a pole, leaned on it, and had a huge dizzy spell. Consuela walked over to him. She had a Navy Blue uniform and pretty black hair and a patch that read "Rodriguez."

"Are you okay, Cooper? Want to lie down?"

"No. I'm alright." *It's the fucking body bags*, he wanted to say; then he did say that to her, out loud.

"Oh." She looked at them with an empathic, fretful concern, then she said, "Try that tent over there. You might find someone there. If you don't, come back and see me." The white tent had the big red recognizable logo.

He walked over there, thrusting his shoulders back. "C'mon, man," he muttered to himself, trying to get composed and talk himself out of despair. "C'mon, man, get your shit together." He entered the tent and walked, almost aimlessly, into a crowd. He looked around.

In a few minutes, someone tapped him on the back. He turned around.

"*Hey*-a Coop."

It was Amy; her face was covered in chocolate ice cream and she wore some kind of paper hat.

"Oh God," Cooper said, dropping to one knee, clutching her by the shoulders. "Oh my God. Amy." His eyes misted up. When he looked up, he saw Mikaela striding toward them with Turk straining on a leash. A Red Cross lady came over with a clipboard; she waited with an official, patient smile.

"Mikaela."

"Shane Cooper," Mikaela said, with a tone that someone would use with "Well if it isn't..."

"You..."

"They picked us up, in the same kind of boat that almost ran us down."

Then the lady with the clipboard said, "Well, you two obviously know each other," nodding to Cooper and Amy. He hugged her and stood up. The lady turned to Mikaela.

"You must be Mommy."

Mikaela's face opened up from its determined weariness; she looked down at her feet and smiled. Cooper walked over to her and hugged her, then the three of them, with Turk, made their way together to the exit for the tent, where the sunshine flooded through.

CHAPTER 51

They walked for almost an hour through a dense, restive crowd, driven by an energy fueled by survival. The ice cream the Red Cross had given them provided short-term fuel to burn. They chewed every last bite of the cones, and were left with fingers sticky with chocolate.

They found a place to sleep. Mikaela and Shane collapsed into an open space with longer grass. A sea breeze blew lightly over everything. They tied Turk up with some old clothesline they'd used as a leash, and left Amy to play with her dolls nearby. Both of them involuntarily passed out.

Cooper woke up in the sun near some picnic tables. He was still in the sway of the anxious dream he'd just had. He'd lost Mikaela and Amy in this huge refugee camp, and while searching for them became lost himself, in dark urban alleys and on escalators to nowhere. He sat up and looked at both of them silently.

"Jesus, that was so realistic," he said.

"What?" Amy said, looking at him critically.

"Nothing. I thought you guys were gone."

Mikaela was still asleep. He thought she looked serene. Amy went back to what she was doing. He found her play, as if nothing out of the ordinary had just taken place, reassuring. She shrugged off trauma, as if it was only the last night's bad dream. It must be the nature of childhood, he thought.

He stood up and took in the vast encampment. It was jammed up against the windswept bay and spilled over into the hillsides and the few streets that weren't flooded. Small FEMA towns–clusters of bland white cubicle shelters–shared the space with Red Cross tents and a vast assemblage of small campsites. It looked like a ghetto, something from Third World disasters.

"I'm going to get more food, from that tent over there," he said to Amy. "Don't move. Keep Turk company." He had to talk to Mikaela, but she was still sleeping. He didn't know what her plans were. He had an idea, but he couldn't read her mind. She was headstrong. Would she want to head to Spokane and look for her boyfriend?

"Don't worry Coop! Right, Millie?" Amy said. "We're not going anywhere. We don't have a car!"

"Good."

She held Millie up so that the doll would do the talking. "But I wanna get out of here. This place is too crowded. We don't have a roof or a house. It smells. I'm sick of this yucky food–mac and cheese and salad, ONLY. Mac and cheese and mac and cheese and mac…"

"Alright Millie that's enough," Shane said, faintly irritated. "It's better than no food, right? Better than floating through the city? I'll be right back."

Just then he noticed Mikaela waking up and moving into a cross-legged position. Her hair was all pressed together on one side, but her expression was gratified and rested. He felt good for her.

"Where are you going?"

"I'm scoping things out, looking for more food, seeing what's next."

"Okay," she said, rubbing the sleep out of her eyes. "I was really zonked out there..."

Amy held Millie up and fluttered her about. "Something other than mac and cheese, please."

"You got ice cream didn't you?"

Then Amy's voice dropped into a mechanical, robotic one.

"More ice cream more ice cream please sir. Please please please."

"I'll see what I can do," Shane said, suddenly feeling like a mildly harried parent.

He walked through the crowd, careful to remember where he left the others. He felt refreshed, almost but not quite aimless. He was over the virus. He heard music, strumming guitars, over behind a tent. A small group played two guitars and one man drummed expertly on an overturned white utility pail.

They had a fire going. Shane quickly scanned the sea of humanity for the signs of a large horse ridden by a tall man in a hat. He was confident that Bea and Drake had made it.

He stood off to the side and listened. A couple of young free spirits were dancing around the fire, Woodstock like. Naked children played; for the moment, they seemed like festival-goers, not victims or refugees.

A man with a beard and a mud-stained T-shirt handed him a leather pouch.

"Have some, dude."

Shane's expression was taken for reluctance, because the man said, "It's only sangria. You have to trust me on that one. Sweet, tangy, and weak. No tequila, Scotch, or fine wine available. It's nectar of the gods. You'll see."

"Okay." He threw the pouch back and quaffed a mouthful. Just as advertised, it was delicious. He took another one and handed it back.

"Thanks. That's really good."

"Pleasure dude."

"Where'd you come from?"

"Oregon, on the coast near Portland."

"Really? Why'd you come here?"

"Road trip. We drove north in a VW van until we ran out of diesel. Then Rainier blows its top. What a trip brother!"

He made it seem like some kind of adventure road trip out of Kerouac or Kesey, but Cooper appreciated the hippy vibe. It lightened things up.

"So going south is out, I guess. Too much traffic. How are you traveling?"

"Don't know yet. Hitchhiking? We're just going to sit tight until we can cop some kind of a ride on a bus or something."

Cooper was half tempted to rally his gang and join this man on the Electric Koolaid Acid Test, but figured it was wiser to keep his options open.

"Well, thanks for the wine. I better be moving."

"Be cool, brother." They shook hands, then Cooper wandered to the next Red Cross tent, where he came up empty, but he found food at the next one.

He took three brown paper bags back to where he found the others sitting on the grass. A woman at the last Red Cross tent, where he found the food, said there were no beds left there, but that they could occupy a corner of the tent if they needed shelter. Cooper looked at the sky, and at the moment it was nice. It was late afternoon and the sun began to dip toward the flat, blue horizon.

The air was clean, cool like autumn. He sat down with the others, and they quietly inspected the contents of the prepackaged bags. He felt lucky and safe; maybe they could leave it to the morning to find out about a boat sailing north.

CHAPTER 52

The bags had turkey, lettuce, tomato sandwiches, and potato chips. Real turkey, even with a slice of swiss cheese with it. They ate in reverent silence, except for Amy who had a faux spat with Millie about her food. She accused the doll of trying to steal her sandwich. Cooper looked at Mikaela with a half smile.

"We can sleep in that tent tonight. Then maybe leave in a day or two. Do you know where you want to go?"

"Out of this place," she said, without leaving much room for compromise. "I heard there might be a train going north. It used to only be used for freight. But they're outfitting freight cars for people, at least according to this guy I talked to. Many roads are out, and there's no gas for cars. So otherwise we're stuck."

"Where's the train go?" Cooper asked.

"Possibly as far as Vancouver."

He launched into his sandwich. For once, it felt like they had options. One thing he was sure of; he wanted all of their options to involve him and Mikaela staying together.

"I thought of renting a vehicle to carry all of us," he said. "I still have my wallet and credit card, believe it or not. I just don't know how soon things will be reconstituting themselves here in Tacoma and Seattle."

He knew he was treading on thin ice. Mikaela wanted to go, not wait for days on end. She'd been clear on that.

She quietly ate her sandwich with her legs crossed, then said "I don't know if the mountain is done yet. We don't even know of it's safe to stay here."

They both stole a wary glance toward Rainier. A gray bulbous cloud, like a permanent thunderstorm, remained hovering over its gouged out slopes.

The sun emerged from behind a cloud, and Mikaela lay back with her hands behind her head.

"I could go back to sleep. For a long time. I really could."

"Feel free to do that. I'll wake you up when the time comes."

Turk sat down beside her, then laid down so his back was touching her legs. Cooper tossed him a portion of a turkey slice, and he caught it in mid air and chomped it down violently.

After about an hour of lolling and napping in the waning sunlight, Cooper came up on one elbow.

"Mikaela?"

She opened her eyes. "Yeah."

"You want to stay together, right? I mean, after we leave here. You're not thinking of splitting up, are you?"

She went up on her own left elbow and faced him.

"Of *course not*! Are you nuts? I wouldn't leave this little muffin!" Then she mussed up Amy's hair, which lay next to her as the little girl fussed around with her dolls in the short grass.

"Thought so. Just asking, you know. Just making sure."

He wanted her in his life; that's what was different

205

between now, and when they were simply clinging to life hour by hour together.

He still heard the music, tambourines, guitars, and singing. Night fell over the camp, which had become like a city on a sweltering summer night. The light blazed in their eyes as the sun dropped into the ocean, then it was gone.

Hundreds of cooking fires, lanterns, and flashlights appeared on the hillsides, like a Civil War encampment.

"I guess we should pull our stuff together and move into that tent. There won't be any space left for us."

"Oh!" Amy said, obdurately.

"We gotta go kid. It's better to have a roof over our heads. Then we'll see what tomorrow has to offer. Maybe we can go, if we hear that this train is running. But we'll need some food, even though it's not that long a walk from here. Ack, let's leave it to the morning to decide."

He was still buzzed on the wine, relaxed and calm for what seemed the longest time since Rainier blew.

Mikaela squeezed her knees together, sneezed, and fell into a phlegmy coughing fit, her head down.

He handed her a water bottle. "I hope you're not catching what I had."

"It's just a cold. Maybe an allergy. It's been a while since I've been able to tell the difference between sick and well."

They got up and wandered over to the tent, Amy and Turk trailing behind.

"What are we *doing*?" Amy said. "Let's go to Disneyland tomorrow! I've never been to Disneyland!"

"Wrong direction," Cooper said. "We have to go north. Some other time though. Maybe we'll go to Disneyland, and the Grand Canyon. I've never been there."

They found the tent and lingered outside with a group of people who were waiting to go in. They set their things down, for the moment, to let the entrance clear.

They heard thunder, and a shelf of murky clouds drifted over the canopy of stars. They ducked under the roof of the tent's entranceway.

Cooper turned to Mikaela, getting something big off his chest. "What are *we* going to do, I mean you and me, when this is finally over? Are you going to go look for Shakir?"

She looked away at the sky, now flashing with streaks of lightning.

"What are *you* going to do, Coop? Head back to Telluride, when the dust clears?" She rubbed her runny nose, as if she was crying. "Go look for your girl, what's her name, the really pretty one."

"Alexis."

"Right, Alexis." She went silent.

"I'm planning on not going anywhere, as in not splitting up. That's a definite no. Maybe we can go to Vancouver together?"

"You want to do that? With Amy of course." There was subtle hope in her voice.

"Hell yeah. I hear the coast is beautiful north of here. Haven't seen much of it."

"I always wanted to see the mountains in British Columbia," she added, a little dreamily.

They hadn't noticed Amy standing between them. "We're all staying together, *forever*? Aren't we?" she said in a high, eager voice, her head craned back.

"You bet."

"And Turk and Millie?"

"And Turk and Millie."

Then the rainstorm rolled in sheets into the camp. They hurried inside. The last thing the region needed was more water, Cooper thought. He watched the sudden runnels of run-off flow past the entrance, some of it stained yellow, as if by pollen, or volcanic ash, or both.

They staked out a 25-foot square segment of the tent interior off in a corner, and huddled together, including the dog. The rain and the wind pounded against the sides of the tent, which bulged like sails in the gusts. At least they had protection, and their bellies were full.

207

Cooper lay next to Mikaela, amidst an unsorted pile of their stuff. He said meaningfully, "I don't want to lose you, Mikaela."

She smiled and snuggled up closer to him, then leaned in and kissed him on the bearded cheek.

The rain pelted the billowing tent sides. She rested her head on his shoulder, and they waited out the storm.

CHAPTER 53

The next day, the rain ceased. They stood in a long line to take short lukewarm showers, with real soap and shampoo. Cooper stabbed at his black beard with an old disposable razor he found lying around, but it was fruitless. He was able to shave up his neck and down his cheekbones, but the rest was going to take scissors, a sharp razor, and lots of slicing and dicing. He longed for a haircut, which surprised him.

It was impossible to make himself handsome for Mikaela, he thought, gazing at bloodshot eyes and a matted mop of dark hair in a cracked mirror. The scabs stood out on his upper body and arms from the various ordeals, particularly his beating in captivity and the scrapes he incurred during the flood and climbing the bridge.

He finished the shower and opened the plastic door for the next guy. Mikaela was planning to take a shower with Amy, so they could both clean off.

The encampment was swampy and morose. Thousands of people milled about the area sullenly, trying to dry out blankets and clothes. A few altercations broke out in the distance, angry shouts carrying over the hills. The gaiety of the night before had vanished.

Hundreds of new arrivals from south of Tacoma and what was left of the Puyallup Valley stood in lines, including older people and grimy faced kids. Mikaela was right, Cooper conceded, the camp was busting its seams and it was time to make an attempt to move on.

Mikaela had volunteered to hand out food, water, and blankets, or anything, but they wouldn't take her. She came back angry at the rigid bureaucracy of FEMA and the Red Cross, and just said, with a bitter hint, "Let's get out of here."

They gathered their things and prepared to move down toward the Port Of Tacoma and the railroad tracks. A line ran north toward Seattle, and certainly into Canada from there. But its availability was all hopeful hearsay.

The passenger trains weren't running, because the lahars and the flooding had destroyed the infrastructure for generating power; sections of track were covered or wiped away by floodwaters or giant mud flows. But rumors ran rife that some of the freight trains were moving and would take passengers. You could go to Seattle, where normal life resumed, where they could be bused away or reunited with loved ones.

Soon, they were back out on the sidewalks of Tacoma, on a hike that Cooper was confident would be a short one. Wandering down empty quasi-residential and commercial streets reminded him of that time in Orting when they ran into Bea. They had about a day's worth of food and water, two tarps to protect them from rain, and Cooper's backpack and bow. He had collected from a Red Cross lady more bandages, tape, aspirin, and ibuprofen for his medical kit.

But now both Amy and Mikaela were sick.

The flood had mostly receded from the city's streets, leaving a slimy residue and a gamey, river bottom smell. The roads were covered with broken glass, and the muddied carcasses of cars that had been carried away in the flood. Shop fronts had been smashed and looted. There was no organized

210

martial law yet, at least in the neighborhoods they walked through now.

Cooper knew he'd be tempted to search the stores. He'd take the risk if they needed supplies.

At one point, he saw a local policeman, with an unbuttoned uniform, his gun belt flung over a shoulder, and striding quickly, as though he was just trying to escape Tacoma himself.

Cooper looked back at Mikaela, who walked behind him with the little girl and dog.

"You know what I'm going to do? When we get through this? I'm going to take you out to dinner. Just us. Candlelight. Maybe an Italian place, a nice one. A bottle of red wine, to start."

"Olive oil, and bread," Mikaela said.

"Exactly. Big goblets of wine."

"A caesar salad," she said.

"With anchovies. Some kind of fancy lasagna."

"Dip the bread in the lasagna sauce."

"Yeah, that's what I'm talking about! A cognac afterward...maybe an espresso."

"A slice of chocolate tort."

"That's right. We'll take hours to finish."

They were quiet afterwards. Mikaela withdrew into her cold. Amy was cranky. Cooper wasn't that surprised; he'd been really sick the week before. And now they'd been exposed to thousands of catastrophe survivors from all corners of the stricken region.

"Amy, how do you feel?"

"Tom, how do *you* feel?" she answered mockingly. "Do you have a headache? Stomach pain?" She waited a moment, then, answering for Tom:

"Starved, yes. Stomachache, no. Tired, yes. Cold, no. Itchy nose, yes."

"Okay, so now that I know Tom's status," he said, looking at Mikaela. "What about you?"

"Just a cold, that's all. I just need a decent sleep."

211

"We shouldn't be long to the depot. Let me know if you need an aspirin."

"I may take you up on that soon. And an espresso."

He laughed.

They crossed a mixed residential and industrial section of town not far from Commencement Bay. They just had to cross a bridge over the Puyallup River, then it would be about another mile to the old Amtrak Station.

This was a part of a city that Cooper would otherwise never find himself in; industrial, polluted, and likely crime-ridden at night. In the best of circumstances. He wanted the group to move faster, but he couldn't push sick people.

He realized the downside of their decision to leave; that now they were passing through a no man's land.

CHAPTER 54

They were alone. The streets were quiet, windy.
Cooper could smell oil and sewage. He could see the cluster of
gray steel oil terminals against the sky, before grimy city streets
ended and the Bay began.

They hadn't reached the bridge over the Puyallup yet.
Amy had been complaining, so they'd stopped and given her
one-half an ibuprofen. Mikaela took two whole ones. They
washed it down with the last of their water. Cooper didn't like
where they were now, wandering through these dead, empty
city neighborhoods. He heard random, purposeless shouts in
the distance.

He armed his crossbow. He heard a transistor radio
playing, as if from an open window. That meant the possibility
of a generator or electricity. Or perhaps, only dying batteries.

Someone read the news on the radio, then the song
"Groovin'" came on. It was the only sound, other than worn
shoes on wet sidewalk.

The streets were lit by a pale sun; nighttime was still

213

several hours off. He relaxed a bit, disarmed and strung the crossbow across his shoulders, and picked Amy up. She acted like she couldn't walk anymore. He was now lugging about 60 pounds.

"It won't be long," he whispered into her ear. Her eyes were closed. Their trudge pace slowed.

After 10 minutes, he stopped at a street corner and set Amy down on some short-cut grass. He pointed to a CVS pharmacy across the street.

Mikaela nodded wanly. She looked pale and sweaty. She sat down on the grass near where Amy lay. Turk wandered over and sat next to Cooper, who scratched behind his ear.

"Want another pill?"

"No thanks, I just want to rest. And get to where we're going."

"Okay, so I'm going to look for water and food in that pharmacy. Turk, you come with me, boy." Both of them went across the street.

The storefront was smashed; glass was everywhere. A BACK TO SCHOOL SALE! sign with boot prints on it lay in the debris. Cooper picked up the dog and escorted him across the shards. Then they both began exploring the ransacked store. "Stay by me, Turk," he called out. He stole a glance out the broken front window and could see the two prone figures of his friends. He'd left the crossbow with the lady, just to be sure.

No one else was around. They headed straight for the refrigerators arrayed along the sides of the store. In the aisles, candy wrappers, chips, and cereal boxes littered the floor. Turk licked at the stale salty crumbs on the floor, which Cooper didn't mind. He didn't see any poison there, and the poor animal was starving, again.

No power meant that all the milk in the glass cases was sour, and the cheese moldy. But he found several small plastic water bottles, which he stuffed into his backpack.

On the far end of the store, a $5 OFF ANY CASE OF 60 OU. PEPSI! sign sat in a heap of empty bottles and trash, but he found one full liter of the soda. He seized that as well, packing it away with other findings: a partially melted Hershey bar, an Orbit package of chewing gum, two cans of dog food, Planter's cashews, and a nearly full box of stale Ritz Crackers.

The only thing of use he found in a flooded freezer was a shrinkwrap sausage that didn't smell yet. He saved it all. Turk clipped alongside him or nosed around some shelves; at one point he lifted his leg on one. *Now I'm really going to get in trouble,* Cooper thought. *This would be the perfect time for troops or patrolmen to come in here, with this dog soiling the looted store.* Loot to survive, he thought, feeling neither high-minded nor particularly competent at getting them to another safe place.

"Sit. Can you sit for one second, Turk?" he said, mildly irritated. The dog obliged, and Shane dashed behind the pharmacy desk for more medicinal loot. The place was ransacked like everything else, and between that and the indecipherable labels, he came away only with one small Motrin bottle and another bottle that contained a run of Amoxicillin antibiotics.

On another shelf, however, he found a battery operated thermometer that still worked. He tore it out of its package.

They went back outside the store. The odd faint music still played on the wind. He gazed up and down the street, sensitive for the presence of authorities whose acceptance of his explanation would be highly unlikely. A group of sickly looking strangers wandered vacant-eyed down the road. They looked over, but none of them spoke up.

Cooper and Turk, who forged ahead obediently, rejoined the others across the street. He found Amy asleep and Mikaela quietly sitting with her head in her hands.

"Take this and squeeze it in your armpit." He handed Mikaela the thermometer, and she quietly did what he asked. Pale and even skinnier looking, she wasn't acting herself, at all.

After a short wait, the little device beeped over and over again. She took it out from her arm and handed it to him.

215

"102.9...and you're supposed to add one coming from the armpit...so you're running a 103.9."

She lay back on the grass and clasped her arms on her stomach. "So that's why I feel like total shit."

"Maybe we should go back to the Red Cross tent."

"All that way? I don't think so."

A man and woman wandered past on the road, like the others, sunken-eyed and shuffling along like zombies. They were clearly from the camp, but the worse for wear from it. They stopped momentarily, and the man mumbled, "You know where there's a clinic open?"

"You might try that CVS store. Over there. It's closed right now, but no one's around. They might have some pills left over. What are your symptoms?"

"Puking, diarrhea, fever..."

"Nasty. I'd check out the pharmacy, then go back to camp."

He kneeled over Amy and felt her forehead; burning up too. He had to wake her, give her an ibuprofen, he thought to himself.

The people shuffled on pathetically. He watched them pause in front of the CVS, the man go in.

We didn't drink any of the free-flowing water in the camp, he thought. *But we took those showers. That might have been contaminated.*

He scanned the nondescript rooftops with their clutter of satellite dishes, and the metallic industrial horizon to the west, but saw no sign of any moving trains.

"We might have to go back to the camp, too." *I'm crying uncle on this journey to a possibly non-existent train north.*

Then Mikaela stood up unsteadily from the grass and summarily declared, "I'm going to be sick." She headed for some spare bushes across the brown grass, but barfed halfway there, hands on her knees. It was wrenching, but not much came up.

"Jesus!" she cried, coughing, half-mad at her body for

216

failing her so.

Cooper came over and put his hand on her back, softly stroking it. She gagged some more, then looked up at him ruefully.

"We're going to have to squat somewhere local." Turk sat a short distance away, curious and concerned.

Mikaela stood up straight. "I may have puked it out of myself. Do you know what I mean?" She spat a few more times.

"Yeah, I hope so."

Then she began to walk and abruptly fainted with a thud as she hit the hard ground beneath the short grass.

CHAPTER 55

Cooper knelt next to her. He let her lie until she was
ready to get up. Turk ambled over and sniffed her gently. He
made a pillow of a few extra clothes and she came to.

"My head?"

"You've got a black eye. Do you have a headache?"

"No."

"You fainted."

"Shit."

"It happens when you have a fever sometimes. Just stay
put for now. I've got some water and Pepsi for you. Amy's
asleep still, but we've got to move into a room soon."

The radio music had commenced. It sounded like an
apartment a block away from CVS, same side of the street.
Stevie Wonder.

"I used to run and ride a lot, and the heavy training
really slowed my heart beat," he said, pulling the liquids out of
his backpack and keeping her mind occupied. "So when I got a
flu, a fever, the blood would go to my stomach and I'd faint.

One time I hit the floor in the kitchen. It's the strangest sensation."

She got up on one elbow and sipped tentatively on a water bottle. "There can't be anything left in my stomach..."

"You still feel really hot. In a while we'll figure out how much you can move."

Stragglers wandered past, but most looked sick and no help to anyone. Cooper knew he couldn't carry her and deal with Amy.

"You might have thrown up the medicine. I can give you more. First things first. Fill up your water bottle with part of this." He handed her the Pepsi liter.

Then he did the same thing; guzzled back some of a bottled water and filled the remainder with Pepsi. He drank it down and it gave him a temporary boost.

He noticed Amy stirring; he handed the same liquid recipe to her. She sat cross-legged in the grass. He opened his kit and gave her an ibuprofen, a whole one this time.

"Do you know how to wash that down?"

"Of course I do! I had to take medicine once. I had a bug in my ear. It really hurt! My mom...she gave me the medicine..."

"Did it help? Your ears?"

"Yeah, they felt okay." She drank from her diluted Pepsi, the bottle tipped up so the bubbles gathered near her lips.

"Don't forget the pill."

"I know I know!"

Same old Amy, he thought. That was good. He took her temperature in a few minutes; 101.1 plus the one, 102.1.

He got out the food, arranging it on the ground. Cashews, Ritz Crackers, a carefully apportioned chocolate bar. He cut up the sausage with his knife, first testing it himself.

He removed one of the cans of Blue Buffalo dog chow and opened it with his Swiss Army knife. It was a painstaking operation, with Turk's nose three inches away and the dog panting and desperately licking his chops.

Finally he pried it open. Having no plate, he wiped off a part of the curb and shoveled the chow out. Turk tore into it greedily and it had vanished in less than a minute. He'd made the dog food seem good.

Cooper saw no need to try to save the food; they needed energy. He and Amy ate handfuls of Ritz, then made short work of the chocolate bar. Mikaela was still lying on her back after nibbling a few Ritz. Cooper made her drink some more of the diluted Pepsi, but she acted really wiped out, worrying him.

Mikaela reluctantly stood up, holding on to Cooper's shoulder.

"This has to be the strangest place I've laid down and chilled in, ever."

"Yeah, right," Cooper said, glancing around the abandoned neighborhood with its graffiti and looted storefronts and distressingly empty roads.

"Where are we going?" Amy chirped, making a short-lived comeback.

"Yeah, what's the target?" Mikaela mumbled.

"Do you hear that radio sound? That's where. The train plan is out. Besides, I don't think you two should travel just yet. We need to sit tight for a day or two, get well. I'm sorry about the train. That was my call. I miscalculated."

"Don't worry. We got sick Coop, not you," Mikaela said gamely. "Wherever we're going, let's go."

Cooper gathered their things and what was left of the food and drink. He put on his backpack, then picked Amy up.

"I can walk!" she shrieked.

"Okay. I'll take you up on that for now." Mikaela began to cross the road towards the broken CVS, one hand unsteadily on Turk's back. She turned back to Shane.

"What do you think we have? What's spreading at the camp?"

"Just some short-term stomach bug," he lied.

He was no expert, but had some training in pathogens from his wilderness responder course. He knew about giardia, which was something that normally struck campers, not refugee camps. He hoped it wasn't worse, like cholera.

"How does it feel to walk?"

"Okay, but I sense an explosion, if you know what I mean."

"I'll get some paper from that looted store."

They stopped across the street in front and he dashed in and emerged with some old newspaper. It came in handy when Mikaela had to duck into some desiccated shrubs and unbuckle her pants and squat.

Cooper watched the road, which had stretched desolately for blocks. Then he saw the horse coming.

CHAPTER 56

It was a black horse, riderless, barebacked, galloping hard. It flew past them on the road, oblivious to its surroundings.

"Wait, I've seen that horse before," Cooper said, staring after it. "The black one that was swimming in the flood, when we were in the boat."

"Poor thing," Mikaela mumbled. "Poor me."

"But where's Napoleon?" Amy asked, one palm upturned, the other clutching Millie. They stood in the middle of the sidewalk.

"Napoleon's probably okay, with Beatrice."

In the same direction came an on-rushing crowd of panicked people. They ran down the middle of the road, away from the same thing the horse was.

"Let's go!" Cooper yelled.

"Where?"

"This way!" he said, turning up the block gripping Amy's hand.

222

The people stampeded up the street, trampling those unfortunate enough to trip and fall into their path. The terrorized crowd spilled over onto the sidewalk.

"What the hell?" Mikaela said over the screams and yells, not quite sure that she wasn't hallucinating with fever. One man stumbled on to the sidewalk and was about to crash into Mikaela and Turk, who barked and bucked at the end of his crude leash. Cooper reached out and blocked the man, gripping fistfuls of his sweaty T-shirt.

"Why the fuck is everyone running?"

"Rats! Millions of them!"

Cooper let him go. He looked up the road behind the people, but saw nothing.

"Total panic, based on a rumor," he said under his breath.

Back into a heavy plodding gait, the man looked back over his shoulder, "You better get your asses out of here!"

A hundred more panicked people stumbled past on the road.

"What is it Shane?"

He looked at Mikaela. "Nothing."

They were walking beneath weather-beaten split-level homes a few blocks past the looted pharmacy. Then he reached the one he was looking for, with a second-floor window open and the radio music softly playing. The old black transistor sat upon a window pane.

"Anybody up there?" Cooper called out, hands cupped over his mouth. Only an organ solo played on the radio, he thought it was The Doors. No other sounds came out of the apartment.

"We need a place to flop, get collected. Let's go!" Cooper strode to the front door and tried the latch, pausing on the stoop. He heard a familiar fluttering, as if coming from a rooftop level. First he looked to the sky, but he saw no birds.

Then he saw large groups of gray, squealing rivulets of fur spread out along an adjacent side street, just behind screaming, running people. The gray rivers moved as if they

223

were one thing.

He tried the next door; locked. He sprinted down the steps and grabbed Amy's and Mikaela's hands and they ran.

"We'll have to try it around back!"

Something had turned the volume up on the fluttering noise. He heard a hideous, deep-throated scream from the street.

An alleyway led behind the building. They ran as fast as sick people could, and when they arrived they found a worn exit door partially ajar. Cooper all but shoved them all inside, where it was dark and musty, and slammed the door shut behind them. Mikaela found a seat on a staircase and put her head in her hands.

"What the fuck was that!"

"Disasters have a way of coughing up the unexpected."

"Sounds like me," Mikaela said, lightly.

"It's gone now. We can try the apartment."

They headed upstairs, Turk now off his leash and leading the way.

They went up a flight of wooden steps; Shane had to carry Amy. The climb was exhausting and painstaking for Mikaela. They reached the second floor. He could hear a muffled, disc jockey's patter from behind a locked wooden door. He called out again, but all the apartments appeared empty.

Cooper smashed the wooden door to the apartment down with the blunt end of a rusty axe he'd found near the rear entry.

They went in and shut what was left of the smashed door behind them. A humid wind blew from the open window; simple furnishings, an empty but swept kitchen. The bathroom still had water in the toilet, but only a trickle came from the faucets. The fluttering, squealing noise had stopped. Shane pulled in the radio and closed the window.

He handed out the rest of the water and diluted Pepsi. They drank quietly. Mikaela had found an upholstered chair and knitted blanket, which she wrapped herself in, even though it was warm and humid. Amy lay on a small couch and guzzled down her Pepsi and then closed her eyes, dolls laying across her chest.

They seemed safe, for the moment. Out the window, the street was nearly empty again. One trampled man stood up unsteadily from the gutter, brushed himself off, and staggered away toward the water.

Shane took Amy's temperature and it had climbed to 104.

CHAPTER 57

"We really have to start taking the antibiotics," he said.
"Yes."

Mikaela looked pale and weak and almost jaundiced. Her eyes were bloodshot, she was collapsed in the chair, and she spoke just above a whisper.

"The problem is, we have only one bottle. And one person is supposed to take all the pills in the bottle. A complete regimen. I think we should try to split it up anyways. It probably will work to kill the bug quickly."

"Give them all to Amy," she whispered. The sun was going down outside, and the apartment had no working lights. The city's electricity was still out. He heard one report on the radio about a hospital vessel and emergency warships and cruisers entering Commencement Bay, and a million refugees in Tacoma, but the batteries finally failed.

Whomever had left the apartment cleaned out the refrigerator. He found Morton's salt on a shelf, with an old bag of brown sugar, and a can of sardines.

"Help will come soon. I saw a helicopter." He did, flying past quickly toward the camp. He still didn't feel good about going back to the camp; Amy and Mikaela were too weak. They'd never make it without wheels. And then there were the rodents. Too many risks. They were stuck, for the moment.

"I think we'll be here for half a day, drinking the water, taking the medicine. I think I made a shitty decision back at the camp. It was my fault. I'm sorry about this, Mikaela."

She shook her head vigorously, "no."

No one came past their building anymore. He heard some dogs barking in the distance and Turk stood by the window, listening.

"I'm going to leave you here with Turk and go back to that CVS. Scavenge what I can scavenge. Are you okay here, for just a short time?"

"Yeah," she whispered. "We'll watch a movie on Netflix." She smiled weakly.

"Jesus, I thought you were serious," he said. "I must be going crazy."

Mikaela closed her eyes again and pulled the knitted blanket back over her head.

He went back to the battered pharmacy. Everything in the store had been rifled and looted. He found more water bottles in a cracked dairy case far in the back, but nothing he could use amongst the medicine, just vials of indecipherable medications.

He returned to the apartment and gave Mikaela two more ibuprofen and some of the new water.

"All I found was the water. I wanted to get medicine for you..."

"I'll be alright...feel better..." she whispered, downing the pills through what was a swollen, sore throat.

"I feel bad," he said. She patted the back of his hand, then lightly gripped it, before falling back against a pile of throw pillows.

He started Amy on the antibiotics. I can control

227

Mikaela's fever, he thought. He was grateful that Amy would take pills, without putting up a fight. Both of their foreheads were afire.

He wished it was him and not them.

He had to move them down to the water where the rescue vessels would dock. But that would take a vehicle or ambulance.

He went up to the rooftop the following morning, scanning for private vehicles he could flag down. Mikaela had spent most of the night in the bathroom. She was running out both ends. She'd be badly dehydrated by now, dangerously. He fed her more water, most of it, but they couldn't keep up with what the pathogen did to her. He was afraid she needed an I.V., couldn't move anywhere.

She would roll her eyes at him gamely, coming out of the bathroom and staggering back to the couch. Turk sat next to her, his tail flipping meekly on the floor.

It was a long day and night. He had a Bic lighter he'd found at the looted store. He attached a rag to the end of one of his arrows and dipped it in propylene glycol. He kept it on the roof; he planned to alert vehicles with the projectile, an admittedly blunt force way to do that.

He went down to the street for long stretches, but the road remained empty.

No fuel or electricity yet, he thought. It was taking forever to restart the city.

Mikaela was not doing well when he went back inside at the end of the day. Amy was sitting next to the armchair crying.

She looked up at Cooper. "She won't answer me. She won't talk. She won't open her eyes. Is Mikaela going to die? I don't want her to die! Is she?" Tears ran down her cheeks, her hair soaked with fever.

"Mikaela's just sleeping. She needs to sleep, just like you. Now come on, back to bed we go. You and Millie have to take more medicine in an hour. Mikaela's going to be okay. Just you see."

228

Amy will be furious with me if I'm wrong. She'll blame me, he thought. *For my inadequacies. For my decision.*

He went back to Mikaela after he'd tucked Amy in. She lay on her side heavily, a trickle of vomit coming from a corner of her mouth. He used his sleeve to wipe it away; she smelled sourly, like turned milk. She truly was unresponsive. He had to hold his hand in front of her mouth to detect breathing. He took her pulse; it was faint and racing.

He held Mikaela's head in his arms. The other sound was Amy breathing deeply. She'd fallen asleep.

"Don't die on me Mikaela. You can hang in there. I know you can. I love you, Mikaela. Don't leave us! Don't leave us now! Not now." He lowered his head and exhaustively sobbed.

"I wouldn't have made it if it wasn't for you. Then I said, leave the camp. Goddammit! I'm sorry. I'm sorry I made us leave. Please. Don't die."

He stayed there and cradled her head as the sun went down. He dabbed her forehead with a wet towel and tried to revive her with a water bottle held to her mouth. Once, her cracked lips moved as if she was talking to him from far away.

"That time my dad was missing, I kept praying that they'd find him. Sitting alone, praying in my room. This feels like back then. Then they told me he was dead. Well they owe me one now. They owe me. *You're not going to die.* You're not."

He'd found a candle and stuck it in a can and lit it. It flickered in the shadows, illuminating Turk curled up next to Amy. From outside, he heard crickets, and engines in the sky.

The next morning, the sun rose over the rooftops. It was clear. A large flock of birds, white gulls, flew towards the sea. He hadn't slept much. He'd heard a couple of cars pass through nearby neighborhoods in the night, but never reached them. *If I ran now I could reach the water and get help. But I just can't leave them,* he thought. *I can't.*

Mikaela was warm, pale, and blue-tinged; barely alive. He went up on the roof and saw three helicopters making their way along the bay. There's still a chance, he told himself. He picked up the bow and lit the end of it with the lighter.

The sun blazed over a brick roof and blinded him.

Minutes later an old blue-metallic car, a luxury jalopy, rolled down the street. He raised the bow, aimed, and fired a flaming arrow. It slammed into the right passenger fender. The startled driver stopped the car dead.

"Hey!" Cooper screamed, waving his arms, one hand clutching the bow. He waved them using the common distress signal, like he wanted to show he wasn't crazy.

"Hey, over here! We need help!" The car idled for a moment. A woman with sunglasses turned her head, the passenger window came two-thirds down. She's looking up in the sun, he thought, she sees me.

I know her.

The driver sped up and began to move away as Cooper waved his arms and screamed at the top of his lungs, "Beatrice! It's Cooper! Beatrice!"

CHAPTER 58

They wrapped Mikaela in a sheet they took off the couch, and Drake grabbed one end. Then they started to carry her down to the street.

"She's heavy," Drake said.

"She's really sick."

"What do you think it is?"

"Something everybody's got at the Red Cross camp."

"Well they say they have a hospital ship docked."

"You're going there, right?"

"Might as well."

"Can you take all of us?" Now they were lugging her down to the first floor and they stopped talking at the first floor landing, until they'd gotten out to the stoop. They put her down for a second. She was dead weight.

Drake had his hands on his hips.

"Well, everybody but the dog I'd say. She can lie across the back seat over a few people, but the dog, I don't know."

"What If I ride in the trunk?"

231

"You'd really do that?"

"Yeah, if you can take the dog too."

"Well then, I guess we're only going a couple miles, maybe five, ten. Let's pile in then. It *is* a Cadillac."

When they'd first pulled the car over to the sidewalk, Cooper had run down and met them. He'd embraced Bea, then brought them upstairs. Bea seemed good.

"Drake took good care of me," she said. "He was wonderful."

"We rode fast ahead of the flood for several miles, then got rained on," Drake said, climbing the stairs. Inside the room, Bea hugged Amy, who led her to Mikaela on the couch. Bea felt around the sick woman's forehead while holding her hand, then she shook her head grimly.

"We need to get her to a doctor, quickly. *Now*."

Soon, they'd all piled into the car and were moving, windows down, to the piers.

They'd convinced Turk to ride in the trunk. They kept the lid lightly open with the rope they'd used as a leash, and he seemed content to lie down on the floor of the trunk and let the air blow over him.

"I have to ask you, where's Napoleon?" Shane said, from the back seat.

Mikaela lay across his and Amy's lap, as still as death itself. He stroked her sweaty brow, and kept praying, praying to himself.

"Yeah, *where is Napoleon? How come he's not here?*" Amy added, pushy and insistent.

"We'd gotten soaked riding in that thunderstorm, and the lightning strikes all around really spooked the horse," Drake said from the driver's seat. "We couldn't take it anymore. I thought Napoleon was going to throw us–they'll do that, you know, if you ride 'em through thunder and lightning," he said with emphasis, glancing back at Amy.

"So I offered to pay this old feller for this car. Just for temporary use. He was holed up in his house. It's a Cadillac Eldorado, you know."

232

"What year?"

"1985. Banged up and dirty engine-wise, but it still drives. It'll get us to the bay. Anyways, if he doesn't just up and lend me the wheels for nothin' but a little cash for the gas, and a promise to return it. The acts of generosity you'll find during disasters, still amaze me."

"But...?"

"I'm getting to that part, little girl. Anyways, I thought Bea and her kindness, and the part about being blind, influenced the old man. I asked him if there was a barn around and he pointed me to a dairy farm up this hill yonder. It still had grass and hills and copses of trees. I left Napoleon there, to run free in a field with a bunch of cows. He'll be alright there; it's fenced in. There's plenty of grass and hay to eat. I'll try to go back and get 'im."

Drake had a city map. They made their way through a warren of streets, pausing at each intersection because the traffic lights weren't working. Cooper held Mikaela's hand. He fingered her wrist pulse at times; it raced along, like his own heart as they tried to make the coast in time.

The crowds became dense as they neared the water. They saw National Guard troops, which must have trucked down or unloaded from a ship. Cooper rolled his window down as they neared a cluster of the guardsmen, grouped on a sidewalk.

"Where's the Red Cross ship?"

They all pointed at once, and one of them yelled out, "Three blocks, that way. Over by the loading docks. Good luck!"

"Thanks! Let's go!" he barked to Drake, who accelerated the car.

After a few blocks, they rolled into the broken asphalt of a service-station parking lot, a half block from Commencement Bay. Cooper and Drake leapt from the car and gently lifted Mikaela out of the back seat. Just ahead, sitting monumentally in its mooring, was a tall, white Red Cross hospital ship.

233

CHAPTER 59: TEN YEARS LATER

Living in Canada, they took a holiday once on a beach near the Olympic National Park outside Seattle. They all liked the ocean, but this was the first time they had been back to the Seattle area together.

The beach was long and spacious, the water frothy with waves and windswept. Shane rented a paddleboard, which he poked around in and mostly got knocked off by waves, which gave him the excuse to swim in the rough but bracing seawater.

They'd rented a little saltbox cottage`that lay at the end of a lane from the beach. It was virtually like camping, but easier and offered a secure roof over their heads.

In the distance, he could see the black form of Amy in her wetsuit, trying to surf. She had long, very blond hair now, and looked every bit the SoCal surf girl, even though they lived closer to Vancouver. She had a boyfriend, and more than a few suitors who pursued the fifteen-year-old at school. She never talked about what had happened to her real family nearby

Rainier ten years ago. Or what had happened to her, what she had seen. She was busy, busy, busy; sports, musicals, and decent at school, a feisty free spirit and a live wire.

In every way, Amy was still the resilient force of nature who people were drawn to, and who he found in that field of flowers so many years ago. Her name was Amy Cooper now. Millie and Tom still lay on a pillow in her room at home with a favorite red blanket.

Shane yelled over at Amy to make sure she was being careful. He was safety conscious and a bit paranoid in that direction; in fact, he was the lead safety supervisor and climber for a utility company in Canada. He only went into the mountains recreationally, when he was almost 100-percent sure he wouldn't be faced with rescue and life-threatening issues. No more guiding for him.

He came up out of the cool water head first, and stole a glance behind him, where the white remnants of another wave rolled along. He went under again to let it flow back over him, and came back up in the sunshine, shook the water off his head, and looked towards shore.

Mikaela Brand sat on a blanket holding their infant daughter, an 18-month old named Shauna. Shane watched his wife stand up in the sunshine, bend down, and set the child down temporarily on a blanket. She began to zip up a black wetsuit, reaching behind her to maneuver a zipper. She pulled brown, very long hair behind to fashion a ponytail, gesturing and he could tell, talking to the wriggling youngster. It would be his turn soon, to look after the kid on the beach, and *she* had her own surfboard.

It was quiet, except for the waves and the wind.

He waved at Mikaela vigorously, until she'd seen him, smiled, knew he was coming in. She hadn't cut her hair once in ten years; she said it was as a kind of testament. To survival.

She was fit as a fiddle as a young mom, now a vegetarian, and wiry. She was an instructor and part owner at a big shiny fitness center in Vancouver. He began to swim to shore with long strokes, stealing a glance over to Amy, who sat placidly bobbing on her board in the sun.

He imagined eating dinner by candlelight later with his wife, Mikaela, only darkness and the plangent wave sounds outside.

When he stood up out of the water, he felt cold and alive. He looked east, toward Rainier, which had a different profile now, more gouged and uneven than the expected curves. The mountain was giant, stately, snow covered, and silent. At least until next time.

THE END